Raising The Pentagon

Three ancient sorcerers caught in a time warp find themselves in 20th century Boston

a New Age Adventure

by

Robin L Stratton

MOCKINGBIRD SQUARE

I would like to gratefully acknowledge the help of several people, including my brothers, Smitty and Jay, for technical advice, Barbara for software exorcism, and Sue Donegian at ZBR. Extra special thanks go to Jim for love and lunch money.

Raising The Pentagon. © 1990 by Robin L Stratton

MOCKINGBIRD SQUARE
P.O. Box 3
Wilmington, MA 01887

√√√√√

Printed in the United States of America

This book is dedicated to Momsey and Dadsey,
not only the two most wonderful parents in the world,
but also the best friends I've ever had.
They taught me how to believe in myself
by believing in me first, and then letting me
take it from there.

"Calurnis boli memnobl Ratrov es keznei."

("Believing in one's power to create Magic
 is essential.")

- From *The Great Book, circa* 900 B.C.

PART ONE

PROLOGUE

" 'Gragulis m xini brui miwu xini
Vyrul zoec roox ga pnenmi-sle
Kouri cwecu m vedlmo omwei bzele...'"

Three hands - small across the palm but long and slender in finger, and deeply etched with lines - reached out simultaneously and sprinkled fluorescent powder into a black cauldron. Thick, dark liquid spit and bubbled angrily over a bright, crisp fire. The sky above was just beginning to turn pink with the first fresh rays of dawn. It was crucial that the Great Ritual be performed and completed before the Great Sun rose at the Great Main Stone of the Great Shrine. Otherwise the Great Spell would be ineffective, and disaster would follow. Probably. No one was entirely sure, of course. No one had ever screwed around with the Great Ritual to find out what would happen if it wasn't carried out properly in accordance with The Great Book of Spells, Rituals, and So On, *which was every sorcerer's Bible.*

"Bni, you always add too much," complained one of the men. His eyes, like those of his companions, were a brilliant glittering blue, with large, pitch black pupils. Also like the others, he had hair that was long and yellowish-white. His fluffy beard completely obscured his Adam's apple - which, incidentally, was not yet called the Adam's apple; although Adam had been dead for a couple of thousand years, the term did not come into general use until the dawn of true Civilized Man.

"You never add enough," countered Bni absently. His concentration was sucked up and absorbed by the bubbles,

9

and he stared into them, mesmerized. His hair tumbled down his back in a mass of almost feminine twists, a foreshadow of modern man's penchant for "permanent" tight curls which, curiously, aren't permanent at all, but need to be regularly reinstated.

"Puu, Bni, stop that," spoke the third man in a voice that immediately commanded respect. "How many times have I told you that it is not the quantity of the ingredient, but the quality of the meditation that accompanies its distribution."

Puu and Bni quieted right down, glancing in shame at one another like chastised schoolboys. Although birthdays and keeping track of one's age were concepts not yet invented, Cozlu had been practicing the Great Magic for longer than either of them could remember. "Bni, resume the chant."

Bni cleared his throat with an important "Hmm!" and picked up where he'd left off, reading from The Great Book *in his clear, musical voice. There was something very pleasing about his intonation, and Puu and Cozlu enjoyed listening to him recite the words. Sometimes Cozlu even shut his eyes in order to hear better (darkened recording studios are based on this very same ancient principle) even though you weren't really allowed to shut your eyes while you were practicing the Great Ritual.*

"'...Hyrudiri xent li mroren
Bakloti ze baklerti...'"

Cozlu's eyes opened slowly and lazily. A vague sense of apprehension was stealing through him, and he took a moment to recognize it and focus on it as he listened to Bni.

"'...Mylenti bishunav m vrend...'"

Cozlu's eyes opened wider, and his mouth, full of tiny yellowish teeth, formed an astonished and frightened "O."

"'...Obla ke nspli...'"

"Bni!"

"'...Xerntra vle griw...'"

"BNI!"

"'Fotor si'- what?"

"Did you say 'Baklerti ov bakloti' or 'Bakloti ze baklerti'?"

"Hold on, hold on," Bni's wrinkled old finger traced up a few lines until he located the one in question, which he read benightedly, "'Bakloti ze baklerti.'"

"You fool!" Cozlu shrieked. "That's the wrong chant!"

Bni and Puu stared at their more experienced companion, bewildered, while a hint of fear crept into them. Somewhere in a tree nearby came the harsh cawing of a crow. That was a bad omen. Something really God awful was going to happen, there was no doubt about it. Alarmed, Bni returned his attention to The Great Book.

"Sneq w fli!" he said, (which is roughly equivalent to our modern day "Holy mackerel!") "You're right! A couple of pages stuck together and I read the wrong spell! Let's see, what does this one do, anyway?"

"I'm afraid you're about to find out," Cozlu answered dryly, looking up at the suddenly black sky with a resigned sigh.

CHAPTER ONE

When the alarm went off I awoke with such a disagreeable jolt that I nearly threw my back out. I could tell I'd be crabby for the rest of the day.

"It *can't* be 10:00 already!" I whined. As a writer, I'm in the habit of rising at a much more reasonable hour - I'm thinking noonish - and could barely drag myself out of my bed, which wasn't actually a bed at all, but merely an old mattress that had recently been discarded by a friend of my mother's.

I stumbled blearily into the bathroom and was confronted by my reflection. As usual, the sight of my face in the morning made me frown. My mirror had a long crack in it that distorted my features which, if the truth be known, are pretty ordinary - resolutely unadorned with any make-up, and set apart from other women only by what I like to think of as my intelligent expression. My eyes looked weary and old and reminded me of raisins in an English muffin. I opened them wide for a second, then let them fall half shut while I occupied myself with brushing my teeth. They're very crooked, my teeth, due to an absence of orthodontic intervention when I was young. It used to really bother me, but eventually I decided that if I was perfectly beautiful, I'd be so intimidating to men that I'd never get a date. As it is, I've worked hard to achieve a kind of "Who cares what I look like, I'm a writer not a model, Goddammit!" ambiance that I'm secretly proud of.

Anyway, as soon as my teeth were brushed I tried to drag a comb through my hair, but it was so long and tangled that I decided it would be easier to shampoo it and worry about the snarls later.

By the time I got out of the shower it was almost 11:00. I was going to have to hurry if I wanted to be on time for my appointment with Elliot Sheldon, my agent. Elliot was mildly interested in my latest novel, *Fish in the Sea*, which was about this woman who is madly in love with this guy she doesn't even know; she relentlessly pursues him, and he finally agrees to go out with her, but then she discovers that he's ignorant, vain, and petty. It's a neat little indictment of society, because the point of the book is that this guy is typical of most of America. I was proud of the premise, and was sure Elliot would be desperate to represent me.

However, I discovered that while he liked my style, he hated the plot.

"How about making it a little more optimistic, Wendy," he suggested as he delicately sipped his drink (mineral water with a twist of lemon - what a trendy jerk he was.) I studied his carefully styled strawberry blond hair, and noticed that his eye lashes were very pale. So was his skin. He looked frail, as if he could be easily knocked over. I was tempted.

"What do you mean," I said. I was nursing a weak screwdriver and thinking about how much I hated getting advice from someone who wasn't a writer.

"Well, suppose you take out all that stuff about society, and make the male lead see how shallow he is? Then he can vow to change. Then he and the main character can get married, and it will be understood that they'll have children - a new generation - who will grow up and make the world a better place. You know. An uplifting message. Something to give the reader hope.

I sighed. I've always hated books that offer hope. I like books that make people think and see. But hope? Nah.

"Elliot, there are nine trillion books on the market today which are exactly like the one you just described. Hope is one of the most commercial, profitable concepts ever invented! We're saturating the public with hope! And what good is it doing? It's doing shit! Know why? Because it's false hope. Because there really is nothing hopeful about society. Hell! We're so fucked up that the best we can hope for is total annihilation!"

I was really pissed. I stubbed out the cigarette I'd been smoking and lit up another one. Smoking is one of the few luxuries I allow myself. Sometimes when I have to make the choice between smoking and eating, smoking wins out. In fact, the only activity that takes regular precedence over smoking is drinking. Not that I have a problem or anything. But frequently I need alcohol to calm my nerves which, because of my sensitive nature, are easily overwrought.

"People like to believe," Elliot went on as if he hadn't heard a word I'd said, and that made me even madder. "They like to think that things can be better than they are."

"But they're just fooling themselves. And we're helping them," I said. If there's one thing I can't stand, it's people who always look on the bright side of things. I mean, I really hate that.

With delicate, feminine sips, Elliot polished off his mineral water, and elegantly signaled the waitress to indicate that he'd like another. His pale, narrow fingers tapped the table impatiently.

"Well, Wendy, what do you propose we do," he said after a moment.

"I say we leave the book as it is. If people don't buy it, then they're ignorant slobs who refuse to face reality." I was going to tell the waitress that I'd like another screwdriver - a stronger one if possible - but she served Elliot's goddamned mineral water and disappeared so quickly that I didn't get the chance. In the meantime, Elliot heaved a deep sigh.

"That's not the way we do things," he said. "We can't afford to take chances like that. We have to have every reason to think a book is going to sell before we agree to represent the author."

"You have no integrity," I said. "You're nothing but a whore."

I glared at him, but he was too sophisticated to let on that he was offended. I saw one of his pale eyes twitch, and his fingers stopped tapping very briefly. That was all. A second later he'd pulled himself together, his fingers resumed their rhythm, and with his stirrer he dunked his lemon a couple of times.

"That may be so," he said, "But I'm a businessman above all else, and I can't afford to worry about integrity. What *is* integrity, anyway? And why do artists always insist that it has nothing to do with making money? Why do they always associate making money with selling out?"

"Because money corrupts you," I said. "Because once you have a lot of money, you get so busy spending it that you don't have time to think about art and improving the world." I felt very snotty saying that, like I was incredibly superior to Elliot, like he hadn't finished evolving spiritually yet and I had.

15

"No," Elliot shook his head, and the highlights in his hair glimmered under the fluorescent lights. "That isn't it at all. You know what it is?"

"For Chrissakes, Elliot, I just *said* what it is!"

"No," he repeated, still shaking his head, now more vigorously - I kind of began to wish he'd pull a muscle in his neck, I've heard that's really painful - "It's because artists are so bitter about the fact that they have no money that they're determined to criticize anyone who does. They want to make anyone who's rich and successful feel guilty. But I don't know a single artist who wouldn't gladly trade in some of his *integrity* for a little fame and fortune."

I wanted desperately to deny that, but I couldn't. All my friends are artists, and whenever we get together we talk about what a kick it would be to have strangers recognize us as we walked down the street or took a flight somewhere or browsed in exclusive cheese shops. Still, I couldn't let Elliot think he was right. So I said in an even snottier voice than before, "Oh yeah, sure."

It wasn't much of a comeback. Elliot certainly wasn't impressed. He just smiled a mild smile and shook his head. I was so enraged I could barely sit still.

"Well," he said, "it's up to you. Either change the story line, or find yourself another agent."

I wanted to leap from my seat, tell him to go fuck himself, and storm off. But I didn't. I just sat there, glaring at him and thinking about all the things I could buy if I could get my book published. My screwdriver was gone, but I tried to sip from my glass anyway.

"I'm going to have to think about it," I said sullenly.

Elliot saw that he'd been more or less victorious and made a halfhearted attempt to disguise a triumphant smirk.

For some reason, that made me madder than anything he'd done so far. Nodding curtly and dismissing the conversation, he picked up a menu and murmured, "Now let's see, what looks good to you?"

Well did he honestly think I would eat with him after that?

"I'll have the chunky ham 'n cheese omelet," I grumbled.

"FABulous choice," he approved. "Think I'll have the Belgian waffles."

I thought, It figures, and I was so annoyed that I longed to slap him. But instead I ate my omelet and listened to him tell me about a party he'd had recently where everyone came dressed as their favorite Shakespearean character and drank wine from a bathtub full of multicolored ice cubes shaped like fish. As soon as I finished eating I told him I'd have to run or I'd be late for my next appointment, and left.

Well obviously I didn't have another appointment. So I wandered around the city for a while, observing the people and thinking about the decision I had to make. I guess, like any artist in my position, foremost in my mind was the idea that maybe I could just this once prostitute myself, do what Elliot suggested, and then, with the money I made, resume my integrity-riddled life, only with a few more comforts.

"But what if the book doesn't sell? Then I will have compromised my principles for nothing," I muttered aloud, scowling to myself as I latched onto a crowd carefully crossing Boylston Street. Even though the sign said we could walk, we couldn't be sure if any of the drivers knew it, so we warily negotiated the oncoming traffic. In Boston you never know if a car is going to stop simply because you're in the road. Sometimes that's just not a good enough reason.

Anyway, I was so submerged in thought - Should I join the   masses of people who were nothing more than

17

domesticated primates doing what they had to in order to survive, or should I maintain my noble convictions even though it might mean starving to death - that I didn't see a guy hurrying in the opposite direction until I slammed into him. The impact hit me the hardest, and while he merely stumbled, I fell right on my ass.

"Why the fuck don't you watch where you're going," he snarled, regaining his balance and rushing past me. He didn't even offer to help me up, or apologize, or anything. For a minute I sat there on the sidewalk, watching him disappear into the crowd and shaking my head in amazement.

"How the hell do you like that," I said, finally lumbering slowly to my feet. Several people had witnessed my fall, and in order to minimize my humiliation, I pretended to be injured. Painfully, I struggled to stand while some passersby watched with friendly sympathy and a little bit of righteous indignation.

"What an asshole," cheerfully observed one, a serious looking young man with shaggy, light brown hair and dark wire-rimmed glasses. He toted a red book bag. His t-shirt indicated that he was a student at Harvard. Either that, or he knew someone who was. Or maybe he just bought the shirt at the Harvard bookstore. His companion, who had black hair and a thin moustache, agreed, and asked if I was okay.

"I think so," I said bravely. With an impressive grimace, I gingerly tested my legs. Then, as they watched, I made a gallant attempt to take a few steps. It didn't really hurt, but sometimes major injuries don't until much later. "I guess so," I said. They nodded and moved off without another word. An elderly balding woman wearing one of those sleeveless cotton house dresses with two big square pockets right in front, touched my arm compassionately.

"Sure you're okay, honey?"

"Yep," I said, "Fine." I saw that she was wearing knee-highs and sturdy brown shoes. She smelled rather strongly of ancient food, maybe an Italian sub. Smiling and nodding hopefully, she waited as I took a few more steps.

"I'm fine," I repeated. I felt so mean, making a judgement about her outfit when she was being so nice to me, and besides, it wasn't like I was any kind of beauty queen myself, that I didn't want to talk to her anymore. "Just fine," I assured her, and turned to leave.

"My name is Myrna," she introduced herself abruptly. I glanced back.

"What?"

"My name is Myrna."

"Oh." I didn't know what to say. Did she think we'd established some kind of basis for a relationship or something? "Nice to meet you," I said. "Well, I better get going, or I'll be late for my appointment."

"Mind if I walk with you?"

"What?"

"I said, Mind if I walk with you. To your appointment."

I said "Um," and did nothing for several seconds but stand and study her. There was a nursing home serenity in her eyes, and her smile, full of uncared for teeth, seemed genuinely kind. I saw that she was wearing this weird amulet around her neck, which was silver and had an engraving of a crescent inside a pentagram. I wondered if she believed it had some sort of magical powers, I mean, that was what it looked like it was supposed to be, magical. She noticed my interest, and wordlessly turned the amulet over to reveal the other side, which bore the image of a chalice. Above that someone had carved the legend, *Pi-job*.

"Keeps me safe," she said.

I said "Huh," and realized that she was still awaiting permission to walk with me. "Sure, if you want to," I said. "I'm not going very far, though." I planned to walk for a couple of minutes, then stop somewhere, announce that my appointment was inside, and take leave of her that way. So with an agreeable nod, I allowed her to fall into step with me. Wordlessly, we headed toward Newbury Street.

"Well, here we are!"

We looked up. I'd stopped at a place called Bauer Wines.

"Your appointment is with someone in a wine shop?" she asked.

I nodded. "Yeah. Going to be right on time, too! Well, see you around."

I gave her a brief smile and turned to go inside. Then I heard her say sadly, "You're a terrible liar."

Don't pay any attention to her, I told myself, She's just a crazy bag lady. But unwelcome guilt had already begun to surge through me, and I couldn't stop myself from turning back to face her.

"What?"

"You don't have an appointment here. You just want to get rid of me."

I didn't answer. I didn't want to bullshit her anymore, because she was obviously a lot shrewder than I'd given her credit for. So I just waited for her to go on, which she did.

"You don't even know me, and you can't wait to get away from me. You can't take five minutes out of your whole life to talk to a lonely old woman. Heavens! What is this world coming to, anyway? Well, go ahead. Run away. I don't care."

Her outburst startled me. I saw there was disappointment in her sweet eyes. I felt so shitty at that moment that I almost threw my arms around her and apologized; but right away I was repulsed by the thought of touching her. It was apparent she wasn't one of your more regular bathers. So I just hung my head, willingly acknowledging my crime.

"Shame on you," she said.

"Look," I said, unable to face her, "I've had a rough day. And I guess I'm not used to having a complete stranger take such an interest me."

"Well, we're not really strangers," she said.

"We're not?" Now I looked at her, curious.

"Oh no. We were good friends in a previous existence."

"Oh." So she was senile after all, and not worthy of my time. I glanced away.

"You don't believe me," she said.

"Sure," I said, "I believe you."

"You think you're so smart," she frowned. "Well you'd be surprised at the things I know about you."

"Oh yeah? Like what." Now I was kind of pissed. How long was this maniac going to keep me here? Meanwhile people were pushing past us, annoyed that we'd chosen to stop and talk right in the middle of the sidewalk. Someone even shoved me. That made me really mad, and I stood glaring at Myrna.

"You're a writer, and you're trying to get a novel published. You've met someone who's interested in it, but he wants you to make changes that you don't like."

I couldn't keep my eyes from opening wide.

"Is that right?" she asked smugly.

"How did you know that? You must have followed me...you must have been spying on me," I accused her halfheartedly.

"Now why would I do something like that," she said, shaking her head. She'd begun to smile at me, and it was a smile completely without malice. Her warm eyes met mine comfortably. She seemed to be saying, "Calm down and listen to what I have to tell you." And so that's exactly what I did. I stood there, in the middle of the sidewalk, staring at her and waiting for her to continue.

"I recognized you the moment I saw you - recognized you from another incarnation. Like I say, we were good friends a couple of hundred years ago. You wanted to be a writer then, too, but you died before you could accomplish this goal. I worked hard to get you published posthumously, but to tell you the truth, you weren't that good, and none of your books sold very well."

"Why are you saying that? It's not true!" I said, unreasonably spooked and upset. I mean, it was really eerie, the way she was talking. Her voice had taken on a kind of mystical quality that disturbed me. I wanted to tell her to stop, but I didn't. I kept listening, mesmerized.

"It was decided that we should meet again in the present incarnation. Once again, the purpose of my existence is to help you. This is because you are an older and more important soul than I. Until I establish myself as a creative, imaginative individual, I can only aid you in your goal. Do you understand?"

I nodded. Don't ask me why. But there was something so compelling about the expression on her face that I couldn't help hanging onto every word.

"You have to keep writing. You can accomplish your goal in this life, but it will take a lot of work. You have to learn to open up your mind. You have spent most of this life being a very closed, hostile, unhappy person. You have also been an unhealthy person. I get the feeling that you've been having trouble with your stomach lately."

My eyes opened even wider. It was true, my stomach had been bothering me. I'd been wondering if I'd developed an ulcer, or if the discomfort was the result of not eating properly, or smoking and drinking too much. And as soon as Myrna made mention of my stomach, I felt it throb painfully, like I'd just swallowed a pulsating basketball. Unwillingly, I thought back on the chunky ham 'n cheese omelet. It hadn't settled well.

"How did you know that," I demanded again, torn between anger and awe. Anger was more comfortable - awe is something I haven't had much experience with.

"Because I am susceptible to your vibrations. I am a very intuitive soul. You are more intelligent, but your intelligence can sometimes hold you back. It fills you with skepticism and it closes your mind."

"You're crazy," I said, but I still didn't walk away. I kept staring at her, waiting for her to tell me more about myself. But she didn't. She just smiled her kind smile.

"Maybe so," she said. "But we will meet again, Wendy. Goodbye!"

She turned and walked away. I didn't try to stop her. I seemed to be incapable of movement or rational thought. Only after she disappeared did it occur to me to wonder how she'd known my name.

CHAPTER TWO

For several minutes I just stood there on the sidewalk, staring after Myrna even though I couldn't see her anymore. In a funny way, although everything she'd said went against everything I'd ever believed, I found myself having trouble doubting her. I caught myself thinking, Wow, I was a writer in my last life, too! and that kind of thing. I mean, even though it occurred to me that I should have seriously questioned her sanity, and even though I have always been someone who needs solid, concrete facts to back up everything, I couldn't help it, I believed everything she said. Maybe I wanted to. Or maybe it was something about her voice, or the wise expression on her face and the knowing look in her eyes. Anyway, I started to wander up the street, thinking about what she'd said, then trying to make my decision about Elliot's publishing proposal, then thinking back to what Myrna had told me, then back to Elliot, then back to Myrna, and so on and so on, until at last I found myself back at my crummy brownstone apartment off Comm Ave. Instead of going in, however, I dug a cigarette out of my purse, lit it, and studied the place. I live in the Back Bay area, which sounds glamorous, but really isn't. I mean, parts of it are.

But I live in a pretty run down section. Next to the building I live in is a fish market that went out of business about eight years ago, and all the signs with all the prices are still up. It kind of depresses people as they walk by, because it makes them realize how expensive fish have become.

I finished my cigarette and let myself in. A gust of hot, unpleasant air hit me, like I'd just stepped into an oven. It was obviously too uncomfortable to stay inside and write. Besides, I was pretty sure I was out of cigarettes. So I left again, and continued up the street until I reached a Store 24.

There was a weird guy hovering near the entrance. He was probably in his late thirties, and his hair, which was very long, was gathered into a thin ponytail at the nape of his neck. His dark beard and moustache were untrimmed. He was one of those leftover hippies that you see sometimes and wonder if they know the sixties are over. As I got closer to him, I looked away. I didn't want to make eye contact with him, because he'd probably ask me for money. But then I figured, He's probably going to ask me for money anyway, and so as I passed him, I allowed our eyes to meet. I was surprised to see that his were glittering with an intense shine. I was even more surprised when he reached out and grabbed my arm.

"Hey, cut it out!" I said, trying to pull away.

"Pay attention," he said, and his voice was low and sinister, "I have been sent to warn you."

"Ow, you're hurting me! Let go! Warn me about what." I was still attempting to reclaim my arm. But as I struggled, he only tightened his grip.

"About the future. About *your* future. You must be very careful. You're going to be in danger very soon. And you must believe in your own powers to transcend that danger, and pull through safely."

I was still trying to get away. People were filing past us,

regarding me sympathetically, but not offering to help. The look in the guy's eyes was really unnerving, and believe me, I don't unnerve easily. But he was staring at me so intently that I was uncomfortable.

"Let go," I said again.

"Just trying to warn you," he said, suddenly sullen. Then he released me and started to walk away.

I should have let him. I should have gone right into the Store 24, and not given him another thought. But instead I heard myself say, "Hey wait. What do you mean, you're trying to warn me? Warn me about what."

He turned back. Again, I was struck by his steady gaze. His eyes were a kind of slate grey. He looked unbalanced, like maybe he'd taken a lot of drugs back in the sixties.

"Really want to know?" he said.

"For Chrissakes, *yes*," I said. I had no idea why I was even wasting my time talking to him. It was obvious to me that he was out of his mind.

"Your life is going to change drastically. You have to change with it. I've been sent to warn you. You're going to be in danger soon. Very soon."

I frowned at him. What the hell was I doing, standing there listening to him? I told him he was a maniac, and started to go into the Store 24.

"Am I, Wendy?" he said, and his voice was quiet and intense.

Well that snagged my attention, alright, and I stopped dead in my tracks. Jesus, how did everyone know my name, was it published somewhere or something? I looked back at him, and saw a slow, sly smile spread across his face. He had me. He had me, and he knew it.

"Got a cigarette?" he said.

"Just going in for some." My voice sounded weak. I felt kind of dizzy.

"Lemme have one when you get out. Then we'll talk some more."

I nodded and obligingly went inside, bought a pack, and returned to him. We opened up the cigarettes, lit a couple, and began to walk slowly back down the street.

"What's going on," I demanded.

He took a long, pensive drag. He was much taller than me, and unhealthily thin. His jeans were torn at the knees and all four pockets.

"It's time for things to change," he said, "and you're in a position to change them. You have the power to turn your thoughts around, and the thoughts of other people, too. But you have to change your attitude, Wendy, you *have* to. It's your responsibility as a writer."

Naturally I was surprised to learn that he knew I was a writer. But of course he'd known my name, too, so perhaps I should have expected it.

"You mean that with my books I can change the world?" I asked hopefully and doubtfully.

"Yes. Not yet. But soon. A lot of different things are going to be happening to you. You have to open up your mind to them. You have to flow with them and learn from them, and then teach others about them."

"What are you talking about, what kind of things," I said, abruptly growing impatient. What was going on today, anyway? Was I wearing a sign around my neck that said "My name is Wendy - tell me something weird" or what.

"Can't tell you just yet," he answered briefly. "Just be ready for it when it comes."

"When *what* comes, Goddammit!"

He stopped walking and so did I. Looking up, I saw to

my unpleasant surprise that we were standing in front of my apartment. He obviously knew where I lived. I looked back at him and saw that he was gazing steadily at me with that disturbing, intense expression. I felt uncomfortable and looked away.

"Believe me, you'll know it when you see it," he assured me with a chuckle I didn't like. Then he turned to leave.

"Wait," I said. He stopped but didn't look back. I heard him say "What." "Who are you?" I asked.

Now he turned around, and he was wearing a friendly smile that made him look almost normal.

"Benjamin," he said, and he even extended his hand for me to shake, which I did.

"Benjamin, how did you know about me?"

"I've been told about you."

When he said that, every hair on my arms stood up, and a chill shot through me. While I pondered his words, he turned once more to go.

"Wait," I said again.

"What."

"Do you know a woman named Myrna?" I wasn't sure why I asked that. It just came out before I knew what I was saying. Benjamin glanced back at me, still wearing that friendly smile, and nodded. Then he wandered off. I watched him go, this time without trying to stop him.

"I've got to stop talking to strangers," I muttered. I smoked another cigarette, reluctant to go inside my apartment. But there wasn't anything else to do. So I finally went in.

I took a seat at my kitchen table and made a halfhearted attempt to work on an assignment my editor had given me, blasting the public's decreasing interest in quality literature. It was part of a series I was doing on the intellectual decline of American society. After a few minutes I'd completed a very rough outline, but couldn't seem to produce anything beyond that. I was surprised, because criticizing society is one of my favorite pastimes.

I had another cigarette and thought about cleaning my apartment. It wasn't really dirty, but by the time it was I might not have time to do it. So I put away my resources, which at this point consisted of nothing more than a stack of those bad tabloids you get at supermarkets, and kind of began to clean. Except for my kitchen table and the one chair, I don't have any furniture, so there was nothing to dust. I can't afford to buy a vacuum cleaner, so I couldn't vacuum. Basically, what I did was make sure the posters of my favorite Existentialists were straight, and I washed a coffee cup that was sitting in the sink. Then I fetched myself a beer from the refrigerator, sat down again, and reached for my notes. But I couldn't concentrate. All I could hear, running through my mind over and over like something in a forty year old black and white Hitchcock film was "I've been told about you" and "We were good friends in a previous incarnation." Over and over. I felt odd about it. Definitely jumpy, and possibly even frightened. I even felt as if I was being watched, and it was a really uncomfortable sensation. My heart was thumping, and I shivered even though I was sweating. Then all at once, determined to face my fate head on even if it resulted in my immediate demise, I flew to the window and looked out. And in that second I was absolutely certain that I was going to see a face staring back at me, I mean, there wasn't a doubt in my mind.

But of course there was no one there.

"I can't stay here," I said aloud, lit a cigarette, and went out again.

I didn't have anywhere to go. I was kind of hungry, but

couldn't really afford to buy myself a meal. I headed across the street to my favorite diner anyway.

Once inside, I seated myself and waited to be issued a menu and my complimentary glass of water.

"Hey, Wendy!"

I was startled when someone dropped into the seat opposite me. Then I recognized who it was.

"Hey, Valentino," I greeted him. We all called him Valentino because he was completely convinced he was the reincarnation of Valentino, the Latin movie star. He knew everything about the real Valentino, when and where he was born, and stuff like that. I was always amazed that he believed in reincarnation, because he was very intelligent. Had a college degree and everything. But he insisted, and none of us questioned him anymore, or even thought about it. "Sell any paintings lately?"

He frowned and shook his head.

"No. I can't even get a showing. No one's into my art. My agent tells me it's too 'obscure.'"

"I love the one you did for me," I reminded him. He'd sold me a painting titled *Prison for the Intellectual*, which was nothing more than a map of the United States. I had it hanging in my living room, right above where I'd put a couch if I had one.

"How about you," he said, glancing at his watch then giving me a really sexy smile. He'd slept with more women than anyone I'd ever met, but he never appealed to me that way. We were just friends.

"Nah, no one is interested in my book, either. My dirt bag agent says it's too 'cynical.'"

"Yeah, well what the hell do agents know, anyway. Hey, Alyssa!"

A waitress approached us. Her name wasn't really Alyssa, I think it was Jean or Joan. But she'd changed it, because she needed an exotic name. When she wasn't working at the diner, she modeled for some of the local magazines. She had dreams of appearing on the cover of *Vogue* and *Cosmopolitan*. Every time I saw her, I couldn't decide if I thought she was going to be successful or not. She was pretty, and she worked hard to keep herself in good shape. But I always thought her face was particularly uninteresting, attractive only in a bland, soap opera way. To me, she looked exactly like every other model I'd ever seen. But she was a good waitress.

"You guys! I've been offered a series of shoots for a suntan lotion company!" she cried.

Valentino and I congratulated her, and as he kissed her, his hand traveled down her back and stroked her waist.

"When?"

She dropped into the seat next to Valentino and leaned forward excitedly.

"Well, nothing is definite yet. But the Browning Tan Company saw some pictures of me and told my agent they were interested."

"Wow, that's really great." I lit up a cigarette and Valentino and I nodded and said together, "Great." I was a little jealous. I always was, whenever I heard about someone else's success. I wondered if Valentino was too, or if he was genuinely happy for her.

"Alyssa, if you don't get off your sweet ass you're going to get fired!" hollered her boss, a nasty old guy who'd tried a number of times to get her into bed. Alyssa giggled and rolled her eyes and shook her head, and her big lime green plastic earrings knocked against her neck.

"I'd like to see him try, the horny bastard," she laughed,

but rose and asked what we wanted.

"A BLT, please, with plenty of B," I said, "and a beer."

"I'll have a beer, too, Alyssa," Valentino said, and his voice lingered over her name. They'd slept together several times, but had somehow managed to remain friends. She nodded and left to get our beers. When she returned with them, we toasted to her good fortune. Then my BLT arrived, and it was full of B, thick and floppy with grease, just the way I like it. Valentino said he was a little short on cash, so I paid. At the door we said goodbye, and he walked off.

Once again I was left with nothing to do. So I decided to go over to Collins Bookstore. I was in the middle of the latest biography of John Lennon, but couldn't afford to buy it until it came out in paperback. Every couple of days I'd go into Collins and pretend to browse, but actually I'd pick up the Lennon book where I'd left off the last time. I was about halfway through.

When I reached Collins, I paused by the window to see if the guy at the register was the one I had a passionate crush on. It was. My skin tingled with exciting chills as I stared at him hungrily. He had long, unstyled brown hair and a beard and a moustache. He reminded me of Dostoyevsky, except that he always looked cheerful. I took a deep breath and went inside. The bell above the door announced my arrival, and he looked up with a smile as I entered. But I was too shy to smile back, and dropped my gaze immediately. It didn't make sense. I've always been comfortable with men; I've always been the type of woman who has more men friends than girl friends. But for some reason, whenever I saw this guy in the bookstore, I could barely breathe. I didn't even know his name, for crying out loud.

I hurried into the biography section, and my heart was

thudding in my chest. If only I could *say* something to him! I agonized as I picked up the Lennon book. But after I'd found my place, I couldn't concentrate on the words. Cautiously, I peeked out around a Danielle Steele display to admire him some more. He was chatting and taking money from a young woman. She was prettier than me, but it was an artificial, careful kind of pretty. Probably without the make-up we'd be about even. Then I saw that she had a little girl with her. Hah, she's married, you creep! I thought, triumphantly; That'll teach you to be in love with someone just because she's pretty! Then I ducked out of sight again, embarrassed by my irrational behavior. That was how I was with him, though - either I wanted to spend the rest of my life with him, or I loathed him. And I had never even met him.

"This is ridiculous," I muttered, slammed the book shut and replaced it, and hurried out without looking at him again.

From there I decided to drop by the office of the newspaper I was writing the article for. I didn't really have any reason to see Blake, my editor, and I knew he was going to give me shit for not having the piece finished. But maybe I could pretend to have a couple of questions about what he wanted. So I crossed Beacon Street, dashing with a small crowd past the traffic that growled impatiently like dogs eager to hunt, and rounded the corner.

CHAPTER THREE

The name of the newspaper I wrote for most often was *The No Frills Dirt*, which never printed anything that was cheerful or uplifting. Other papers called us "The Bitchin' Rag," not because we were cool in the 1950s sense of the word, but because all we did was complain about the state of society. Well someone had to, right? I mean, sure, it's fun to write about the latest exploits of Cher and Madonna and the Royal Family, but our paper just didn't have the time for that fluff. We had *serious* shit to worry about, goddammit. We offered brutal journalism, pointed fingers at officials in high places, and praised the artistic quality of eras gone by.

As I entered the office, Blake looked up from the mountain of junk piled on his desk. His dark glasses were shoved to the top of his head, his sleeves were rolled up as high as possible, and I saw that the wastepaper basket near the filing cabinet was overflowing.

"Finish your piece?" he greeted me hopefully. He was sweating profusely. The *No Frills Dirt* office couldn't afford air conditioning, and the fan at the window had to be turned down low so as not to disrupt the papers on the desk.

I shook my head frankly, and Blake sighed.

"Got a deadline to meet, you know," he said.

"I know. I'm sorry."

"Having problems? Can't find resources, or something?"

"No, it isn't that." I picked up a stack of advertisements from a chair, set them carefully on the floor, and sat. "I guess I'm kind of having trouble concentrating on it today."

"Oh that's right - you had an appointment with your agent this morning. How'd it go."

I smirked and shook my head.

"That bad, huh? What happened."

I told him what Elliot had said. Blake nodded. He had a very serious, stern expression on his face. His sloppy, greying hair was parted somewhere at the side, and he kept running his fingers through it - something he always does when he's annoyed. I knew he was going to tell me that Elliot's proposal was preposterous. And sure enough, he sat back flipped his hand as if to dismiss any notion I might have of changing my book.

"Don't do it, Wendy. Don't be part of the herd."

I nodded, but felt compelled to justify my indecision.

"It's just that I'm so broke. And you know how hard it's been for me to even get an agent to agree to read my manuscript. This might be my last chance."

Blake and I lit up simultaneously, almost absently, and began to smoke hard.

"Would never being published be so terrible? Would it be worse than betraying the values that are so important to you?"

I saw it was useless to argue with him. It was easy for him to say "Don't do it," because his wife Anne had a high paying job and he never had to worry about trivial things like eating and having a roof over his head. I heaved a sigh.

"I don't know," I said.

Blake shuffled through some papers on his desk until he came upon an envelope, which he handed me. Inside was a four page article titled "Time for a Change."

"What's this," I murmured, not waiting for an answer as I scanned the article. The author, Scott Bedford, was urging readers to "Stop and examine" their own thoughts. He said it was our responsibility to improve the world, that it wasn't going to get better all by itself.

"This doesn't fit in with our format," I objected. "You're not going to publish, are you?"

"Sure we are. In our own way."

"What does that mean?"

"We'll print it. And then we'll print a rebuttal. This guy's just a naive jerk, Wendy. He seems to think we can create some kind of utopia here, if we just set our minds to it. Jesus! If only it were that simple! But he's not taking into account some teeny weeny considerations...like a hopelessly corrupt government. We've got to present his letter as an example of how *not* to think. We'll make people aware of the ignorance and naivete, and even the danger of believing we can peacefully coexist in our society's state of intellectual decline. Look, this guy Bedford is espousing all the wrong priorities! He says to 'believe, above all else.' What the hell does that mean? Believe in what?"

"So you're going to blast the piece."

"Bet your ass."

"Serves the cheerful bastard right," I nodded, but my heart wasn't really in it. I was still reading the article.

"The time is now! And it's up to us! There is no other option if we're going to make this thing work."

"Shit," I said. "He writes like a kid who's never suffered."

"I know. Obviously *The No Frills Dirt* has nothing against improving the world. But going around believing in everything isn't the way to go about it. In fact, that childish attitude can actually be a hinderance to the ultimate goal. Hey, I like the way I put that. Be sure to use that in your rebuttal."

"*My* rebuttal?"

"Sure. This one's yours. I want you to give this guy Bedford all you've got. Let him know we applaud his enthusiasm, but show that he's hitting the nail on the sharp end."

One thing I always liked about Blake was that he would take a common cliché, and switch around to make it mean just the opposite. He was a good newsman.

I went back to reading the article. Scott Bedford was optimistic in a really aggravating way. He was saying that all we had to do was change our thinking pattern - start having confidence in our own powers - and everything would be just fine. Blake was right. The guy didn't know diddly shit about pain or reality.

"I'll cream him," I promised.

"Good. Take a break from the other piece, the one about quality literature," Blake said. I nodded, slid the article back into the envelope, then put the envelope in my purse.

"Well, see you," I said.

"Give him hell, Wendy. And that asshole Elliot, too."

I was frowning as I left the *Dirt* office and walked back into the bright, hot sun. This was the sixth or seventh day in a row that the city had been oppressed by a desperate heat. All over, the sick and the elderly were dying of it. Even worse, the rich people were being asked to turn down their air conditioners because of the electricity required to run them.

37

I wasn't ready to go back to my apartment yet, so I decided to take a long walk and think about everything that had happened that day. I was feeling kind of funny, the way you do when you're anticipating something new. I felt like something major was going to happen to change my life, and I was a little apprehensive about it.

I walked until I reached the Public Garden. Bums slept in the sun while the usual street musicians performed before unenthusiastic audiences. Someone handed me a pamphlet that said "Need a friend? Turn to Him," which I dropped into the next trash can. A couple of kids on skateboards flew past me, and I cursed them as I scurried out of the way. An old guy sweating in a flannel shirt and a coat asked me for money. I said, "Sorry, I'm a writer," and he backed off.

Pretty soon I reached the pond where Boston's famous Swan Boats were majestically moored, and as I watched, a couple of dozen people boarded. Children were all over, squealing and giggling and trying to get away from their parents and run closer to the water. There was a lot of parental screaming going on - "Billy! Come here!" "Young lady, get away from there!" - that kind of amused me. I wondered what it was that made people actually want to have kids. I never intended to have any myself.

Eventually all the parents had herded their children aboard, and the huge swans began to move forward slowly. I went over and stood on the bridge to watch them pass below. The children were all quiet now, subdued by the unfamiliarity of their adventure. One caught my attention, a kind of serious looking little boy with glasses. His eyes were devouring the scenery, and I looked around and tried to see things as he was. I saw trees thick with leaves and a vivid blue sky. Some people walking by held helium filled balloons with smiley faces on them. Nearby, a couple was making out in the grass. I looked back at the boy, and he was watching some ducks that were swimming near the boat. He pointed them out to his parents, and they smiled and nodded at him. But before I could even feel good about the scene, it occurred to me that the world might really suck by the time he grew up. It was a sad thought. I recalled my own childhood, and the house where I used to live. We had a big yard full of trees, and the water and air back then was a lot cleaner. What if the world was one huge parking lot by the time this kid graduated from high school? What if the world wasn't even around anymore, what if we'd blown ourselves up? He'd never have the chance to grow up and have kids of his own, I thought.

A tap on my shoulder startled me. I turned to see Benjamin standing there, smiling and squinting in the bright sun.

"We meet again," he said.

"Yeah," I said.

He leaned against the bridge and watched the Swan Boats with me for a moment in silence. There was a musky, earthy smell coming from him that wasn't altogether unpleasant, but I wouldn't want to smell that way myself. I waited for him to speak.

"You know," he began, and his voice was very gentle, "back in the sixties we had a lot of hope for the future. I know that a lot of people think of the sixties as being a time of drugs and sexual promiscuity. Well, it *was* that, but it was more than that. We talked about love, and we assumed that with this love we could change the world. We were the children, the world was ours, and it was up to us to keep it beautiful. Our parents had fucked up, and now it was our chance to fix things. And we tried, we really did."

His eyes met mine, and there was an urgency in them that surprised me. I wondered just how insane he was. I wondered if maybe I should just walk away. But I didn't. I nodded sympathetically, and waited for him to continue.

"I don't know. I'm not sure what happened. But after college my friends got high paying jobs, and all of a sudden they didn't give a rusty fuck about love, or peace, or the environment. All they care about now is making as much money as they can. I worked for a while, too, but I couldn't deal with it. There's too much hypocrisy out there. So I just quit. I haven't had a job in ten years."

He heaved a sigh and stared morosely out across the water. The Swan Boats began to make their way back. I didn't know what to say. I felt sorry for him. But I just couldn't think of anything to tell him that would make him feel better. And abruptly, he resumed speaking, this time with a passion that impressed me.

"You know what the problem is, Wendy? The problem is, we've been taught to believe that we're powerless. We've grown up thinking that we're too small to change things. And as a result, we've lost hope. And without hope, we're really fucked."

Again he fell silent. As the two of us watched, the Swan Boats came to a halt, and everyone began to climb out. I couldn't help but be reminded of the childish article I'd just read by Scott Bedford.

"Yeah, but," I said, "basically we *are* powerless. I mean, I see the shit that's going on. But what can I do? What can one person do?"

Benjamin looked a me for such a long time that I became acutely uncomfortable. His disappointed eyes bore into mine, and I finally had to look away.

"Yeah, I guess you're right," he said quietly, "I guess you may as well not even try."

And he turned to go. I called him back - I'm not sure why - but he didn't even turn around. I heard him say, "See you later, Wendy," and then he disappeared into the crowd. I tried to be pissed at him for walking off like that, but I couldn't. For some reason, I felt ashamed. I watched the next load of people board the Swan Boats, and then I headed back to my apartment.

CHAPTER FOUR

The phone was ringing as I let myself in. I scrambled over to it, but then didn't pick it up right away. If you want to know the truth, I was a little spooked. It had been such a weird day. There was no telling who would be on the other end. When it rang again I forced myself to answer it, and my voice sounded timid as I said, "Hello?"

"This is Collins Bookstore. The book you ordered is in."

My mouth dropped open. Collins Bookstore! That was where the man of my dreams worked! But was this him? Or was it just some other guy who worked there? I'd never spoken to him, so I couldn't be sure. I'd heard him make calls like this one. But why would he be calling me? What had he just said?

"Hello?" said the voice.

"Yes, I'm here! What did you say?"

"The book you ordered - *Creating The Magic Within Yourself* - is in."

"I didn't order that book," I told him regretfully. Then, desperate to keep him on the line in case it *was* him, I asked what the book was about. My heart was still thumping. I put my hand over it as if to calm it.

"You didn't?" There was confusion in his voice. "Is this..." he read off a number that was similar to mine, but was off by one digit. I explained this to him, and he apologized.

"Well, in answer to your question, the book is about...wait, let me read the cover...'*Creating The Magic Within Yourself*...How to change your life through believing in yourself.' It's about having confidence in yourself and your dreams. The author says that if everyone read the book, it might lead to world peace."

I just said "Huh." Last week it wouldn't have interested me at all, but it seemed to tie in with what had been going on that day. It struck me as being too much of a coincidence not to mean anything. Besides - he sounded as if the book intrigued him. So I asked if he'd read it.

"Not yet, but I'm going to."

"Maybe I will, too. Is it expensive?"

"Well, kind of. It's pretty thick. Hardcover."

"Oh."

"I ordered a couple of copies of it. Why don't you come in sometime and take a look at it?"

"Okay," I said, and I felt shaky and weak.

"Good. I'll see you later, then," he said, and we hung up. I collapsed on the floor still holding my hand over my heart, and thought about the first time I'd seen him.

It was about seven months ago. I was dating a building inspector named Phillip. He wasn't particularly exciting, but I stayed with him for an entire year because there wasn't anyone else I wanted to go out with and because I was bored. But then he started to get on my nerves with his annoying little habits, particularly his penchant for keeping me updated on his mileage. He'd say, "Today on the way over here my mileage was 86,866.6." Eventually I realized I was more bored going out with him than not going out with him, and that was when I broke up with him. But instead of taking it like a man, he cried and begged me to marry him. So I told him I'd think about it, and headed straight for Collins Bookstore. I always go to a bookstore when I'm upset. I don't know why, but I always think I'll find a book that offers advice for the very problem that's upsetting me. It's like those people who turn to the Bible whenever they're troubled; they open it at random and arbitrarily choose a passage which they read and try to relate to their circumstances. Pretty superstitious. As if Whoever is in charge of the universe has time for that kind of thing. Nevertheless, it's what I always do, and it's what I did that day. I went in looking for a book about what to do when an incredibly boring man asks you to marry him. Instead, I found that Vinnie, the old manager, had been replaced by a new guy with eyes that were very warm and brown. Something inside me went ZING! and my legs felt wobbly, like they were going to quit supporting me any second. The new manager smiled at me, but I couldn't smile back, I just turned around and walked out. Then I called Phillip and told him we were through.

So after seven months of being passionately in love with this guy, was it any wonder I was incapable of movement? For a long time I sat there on the floor, still holding my hand over my heart, thinking back on everything he'd said. What kind of man would be interested in a book about magic? I wondered. Was he really so gullible? Maybe it hadn't been him after all, maybe it was someone else who worked there. I went over his words over and over. But pretty soon my back got cramped and I had to stand. Glancing at my clock,

I saw that it was as good a time as any to eat dinner.

I consulted my refrigerator. Olives, butter, a partial loaf of white bread, and plenty of beer. As usual, my most promising option was a peanut butter sandwich.

While I ate, I prowled around my tiny apartment, going over the outline I'd written, and glancing out the window. I still felt nervous, like something strange was going to happen any minute. I read Scott Bedford's article again, but I couldn't concentrate on it. Finally I just shoved it back into the envelope, dropped the envelope into my purse, had a quick cigarette, and went out.

I had no place to go. I stood in front of my apartment, contemplating my options. It wasn't quite dark out, so it wasn't completely dangerous for a woman to be alone in the street. Still, I would have preferred to hook up with a group. I needed to talk to people I knew and was comfortable with to take my mind off my uneasiness.

After a second, I lit up another cigarette, and started up the street toward Max's, a club I go to a lot. On the way I passed Collins Bookstore and looked in the window, but there was a woman at the register, and no sign of my guy. So I kept going.

Max's was jumping by the time I got there. A dj was playing a Springsteen tune that had everyone on their feet. It was kind of dark inside, and so smokey you couldn't see clearly more than ten feet in front of you. What I liked best about Max's was that all the walls were plain, and patrons were welcome to scribble graffiti anywhere they wanted. You'd probably expect to find a lot of profanity there, but for some reason, people were more apt to quote poets or leave cryptic and often cynical messages. It wasn't anything like what you find in department store bathrooms. I'd written some things myself, my favorite being a line from Hesse's *Demian*: "Sinclair, the majority's path is an easy one, ours is difficult." I went up to the bar and ordered a beer, then surveyed the crowd, hoping to recognize someone.

"Wendy! Hey, Wendy!"

Just barely above the din I heard someone calling my name. I spun around, saturated in relief. A guy about my age was pushing his way amicably through the crowd, smiling an apology to all.

"Rich!" I greeted him with an enthusiastic hug. He was just the person I needed to see. Unlike most of my friends, he wasn't an artist. He was an ice cream man. I liked to visit him because his freezer was always stuffed with juice bars and Italian ices and snow cones. He drove around town in his ice cream truck, even when he wasn't working. Even when he had a date. Sometimes women were embarrassed when he showed up in his "Mr. Happy's Cold Stuff" vehicle, and sometimes they even refused to go out with him. But he always said that if they cared about stuff like that, then they weren't worth his time.

As he returned my hug, his pink face was lit with pleasure. He was so uncomplicated that he liked everyone; he saw the good in everything. I had no idea why. He was very sentimental, too. Once when I was visiting him, he was watching *The Sound of Music*, and he started to cry as soon as the Von Trapp children began to sing for the Baroness.

"C'mon over here and sit with us," he invited, leading me to a table he was sharing with a few people I knew fairly well. We all exchanged greetings, and I sat in the only empty sat. Lighting a cigarette, I picked up the threads of the ongoing conversation.

"The problem with today's society is that no one

taking a long, painful sip.

"Feel as bad as you look?" I inquired sympathetically. But he didn't answer, he just stared morosely into the mug.

"What happened last night," he said finally.

"Nothing." I reached for my cigarettes, then offered him one. We smoked in silence for several minutes. Eventually I asked him if he'd like toast or something. I hoped he wouldn't want "something," because like I said before, toast was his only option. I should have offered him "toast or nothing." He shook his head, glanced at his watch, and said he'd have to hurry or he'd be late for an appointment. Since I had used that same line myself only the day before, it sounded pretty fishy to me. But I nodded and said, "Okay." I wasn't all that anxious to have him stay - now that it was light out - because suddenly we didn't seem to have much to say to one another. He finished his coffee and his cigarette, went into the bedroom, and returned dressed.

"Well, see you," he said, tousling my hair as if I were an obedient dog. I didn't say anything as I watched him go, and then I poured myself another cup of coffee and tried to decide if I wanted to feel shitty about the situation. I thought about my guy at the bookstore. I wondered what he'd done the night before. I wondered if he had a girlfriend. I tried to picture what he'd be like after a night of passionate love making. I pictured him waking up first, shaking me gently, and telling me tenderly that he couldn't live without me. As I lit another cigarette, I noticed it was my last.

"I've got to change my lifestyle," I said.

I worked for a little while on the Scott Bedford rebuttal. I'd read his article so many times that I practically knew it by heart. In a funny way, the more I read it, the less it offended me. As a matter of fact, I even started to feel a kind of affection for him. He was so full of goodwill, like a Christmas carol, that it was going to be difficult to attack him. Still, his ideas were juvenile, there was no denying that. I mean, he actually thought that all people had to do was believe. For him it was that simple. Slowly and methodically, I began to tear him apart.

I'd almost reached the end of my first draft when I looked up and noticed it was after 5:00. Time for dinner. I recapped my pen, stood, stretched, and prepared my meal. That took about a minute. I licked the peanut butter off the knife, ate the sandwich, and before I knew it, it was almost five minutes after five. I reached for a cigarette, but the pack was empty.

"Shit," I said, mildly upset. "Guess I'll have to go out." Then I remembered that I was going to go to Collins to pick up the book about magic. It seemed kind of silly, buying a book I didn't want when I was so broke. But it was in the name of love. So I jumped in the shower and washed my hair and even tried to style it a little. If I was going to meet my bookstore guy I wanted to look good. Well, that is, as good as I could look, which wouldn't be pretty, but would at least be okay. Besides - my bookstore guy wasn't so shallow that he'd go out with a woman because of her appearance. He had more depth than that. But at the last minute I discarded my jeans and my "Life sucks and then you die" t-shirt in favor of a short, tight dress some guy gave me a few years ago.

I wanted to get cigarettes first, but as I headed toward the Store 24, I wondered if Benjamin would be there again. I didn't feel like seeing him, because I didn't want him to unnerve me. So I decided to go to Collins first. My heart was throbbing. Was I going to make a fool of myself? My pace slowed. I rounded the corner and saw the sign. Collins

Bookstore. Taking a deep breath, I peeked in the window. He was there! He was at the register! I had to step back to collect myself. I thought of my sordid activity the night before, and felt shitty. When I looked at him again, he was waiting on an elderly man, chatting with him and leisurely counting out change. He's so polite, I love him so much! I thought frantically. As I prepared myself to go in, the elderly man held the door open for me. But I couldn't thank him or even look at him. I just flew past him to hide behind the biographies. As I snuck a glance at my bookstore guy, I felt as if my heart would explode with schoolgirlish adoration. Most of the other customers in the store filtered out, and he turned his attention to a book that was lying open near the register. He was leaning over with his chin buried in his hands, deep in concentration. I loved him very desperately. I have to go over there! I thought, I have to ask him about the book! But I was having trouble moving, and not only that, all at once it occurred to me that it might not have been him who called me. What if I went over there and asked him about the book, and he didn't know what I was talking about? I'd look so silly that I could never come back, and then I'd never see him again. I stood very still for a long time, staring at him and hovering in the biography section. With one finger I tapped a thick book about the Kennedys and the Fitzgeralds, and thought, What should I do? What should I do?

Then all of a sudden he stood up, stretched, and noticed me standing there.

"Help you find something?" he asked, and his voice was gentle and friendly. Luckily I was unable to move, or I would have ducked out of sight. I just stood there, gazing helplessly at him.

"Are you looking for something in particular," he revised

his question, hoping to get some kind of response from me. I tried to answer, but couldn't. Instead, I heard myself ask him what he was reading. He looked down at his book, and his face brightened.

"It's a book about magic."

My body sagged with relief. So it *had* been him! As I somehow found the courage to approach him, he went on, "It's really interesting. According to the author, thousands of years ago there were these sorcerers who could influence the weather and heal people and communicate with animals. He said the reason these sorcerers were so powerful was because they *believed* they had power."

"Really?" I was doubtful, and it showed. I hated to disagree with him so soon in our relationship, but I couldn't help it. Now I was standing near him, and up close he was breathtaking. His hair badly needed trimming, and I liked that because it meant he probably wasn't vain. His nice brown eyes were full of benevolence.

"Well, the author provides plenty of names and dates, and he seems to have done quite a bit of research. And he's not just some uneducated schmuck, either - he has Ph.D.'s in Astronomy, Physics, and Archeology, and he's mastered about a dozen ancient languages. Went to Harvard. Lives right here in the city."

"Really?" I said again, only now I was kind of intrigued. "Tell me more about the sorcerers."

"Well, apparently there was this ancient handbook that was passed from generation to generation and it was full of spells. It seems that even after hundreds of years, the book never wore out. And this guy believes that it still exists somewhere, still intact."

"And the sorcerers used that book to make magic?"

"Yeah. It was always a trio of sorcerers - a teacher and his two students."

"Why two?"

"In case something happened to one. See, it wasn't like a course that just anyone could take. When someone was chosen to learn sorcerery, he devoted his entire life to it, and took over when his teacher died. You couldn't just go out and find a replacement, so you always had to have one in reserve."

"Oh."

"Anyway, these sorcerers were so convinced they could do anything, that they never questioned their ability. That's the point of this book - in our society we're so skeptical that we limit ourselves. This guy says it's time to open up our minds and recognize the power we all have within."

"And you believe that," I said carefully.

He smiled a little sheepishly. I didn't want to be mean, but I've always been impatient with people who are gullible.

"I don't know if I do or not. It probably doesn't sound very credible when I say it, but you might feel differently if you read the book. The author says it better than I do."

He looked at me hopefully. I wanted to nod eagerly and say, "Oooh, I believe it all, too!" but that just isn't the way I am. I need a lot more proof than just somebody's say so - I don't care how many Ph.D's he has.

"What's his name," I asked on the outside chance that I'd heard of him.

"Dr. Mason Holdsworth. You know, he didn't believe in any of this at first, either. He was studying ancient superstitions - he'd been contracted to write an article. But then he got caught up in the research and wound up traveling all over the world. He spent the last sixteen years working on this, compiling all he learned. He said that the knowledge changed his life."

"The knowledge?"

"Of believing in his own power and his own ability to perform magic. In the book he gives a couple of examples of times when he cultivated such a firm belief in something that it came true."

I didn't say anything for a minute. It sounded so far fetched. But it had really set my bookstore guy on fire. I admired the way his eyes were lit up with passion. I wanted desperately to believe with him. But magic! Jesus.

"Look," he said abruptly, "I'm almost done with this. Why don't you stop by tomorrow and borrow it? You're in here all the time anyway."

A warm flush spread across my face. He'd noticed me!

"Well, okay," I said.

"I'll be interested in hearing what you think of it. What's your name?"

"Um, Wendy Jenkins."

"Hmm, that sounds familiar." He studied me so carefully that all of a sudden I was sure he knew that I was in love with him, and that I couldn't have cared less about borrowing his silly book about magic.

So I said quickly, "I write for a local newspaper. Maybe you've seen my name there."

"Maybe. What paper?"

"*The No Frills Dirt.*"

"I've heard of that," he said, and there was a tiny, amused smile on his face.

"What's your name?" I asked.

"Scott Bedford," he said.

PART TWO

PROLOGUE

Cozlu was the first to return to consciousness. He blinked reluctantly several times. Then with a painful grunt he struggled to sit up, and looked around. The surroundings were completely unfamiliar. Swallowing his alarm, he occupied himself with rousing his two companions, who lay face down next to him.

"Bni, Puu, wake up now."

Bni and Puu squinted, resisted Cozlu's command at first, then eventually came to attention and sat up.

"What happened? Where are we? What's going on?" Bni wanted to know. He was staring in disbelief at everything, from the huge, shiny structures that blocked out the sun, to the multicolored objects that hollered past them.

"I don't know," Cozlu answered grimly. Bni and Puu stared at him, then at each other.

"You don't know?" Puu echoed. Then all three gasped, astonished, to see a gigantic metallic bird roar across the sky above. "What was that?"

Cozlu shrugged with brutal frankness. He tried to think of something to tell them to alleviate their fear, but he was scared, too, and couldn't think of anything to say. So he just looked around some more at the strange place they'd traveled to. They seemed to be in some kind of small, enclosed field, with small sparse patches of grass here and there. In the center of the field was a pile of wood that had been cut into straight, flat pieces. Apparently they'd all fit neatly together at some time, but had since been torn apart. Weeds had begun to grow on the top of the pile. Cozlu found it very unsightly, and wondered what its purpose was.

"But what will we do? What will happen to us?" Bni leapt to his feet as if he had intentions of scurrying off to somewhere safe. But of course he knew of no such place. So he just stood, wringing his hands like an old woman, and waiting for Cozlu to come up with some kind of solution.

"Cozlu, what was the spell Bni cast?" Puu demanded, covering his ears and wincing at the horrible, loud sounds. "What has he gotten us into?"

"Well, the chant Bni recited was a time travel ritual."

The jaws of Bni and Puu dropped open simultaneously.

"You mean..."

"We're in a different time?"

Cozlu nodded sourly, and rose to his feet. He was trying to maintain his calm, but being transported several thousands of years into the future was a major inconvenience. He'd heard stories of it happening, but he'd had no personal experience with it himself. Nor had he, in any of the stories, heard of anyone returning safely. It was a nasty situation.

"What should we do?" Bni and Puu asked together. Puu had risen, too, and the three of them stood in a triangle - tiny old men with white hair and brilliant blue eyes. And dressed, of course, in ceremonial attire - bright blue robes with yellow stitching, tall pointed caps, and sandals.

"I guess we should try to find our way back," Cozlu said. And so they began to walk.

60

CHAPTER ONE

I hurried out of the bookstore and went back to my apartment to study Scott Bedford's article again. Shit! Didn't it just figure that the man of my dreams would turn out to be an idealistic fool? I wanted to cry. No wonder he was always smiling and so cheerful to his customers - he was living in a dream world he'd created! I thought about Benjamin, and how dissatisfied he was with everything. Suddenly I hoped I'd see him again, suddenly I felt like I needed to talk to someone who wasn't blind to the problems of society.

Jamming the article back into the envelope, and the envelope back into my purse, I left my apartment right away, heading for the Store 24. I didn't see Benjamin anywhere, but as I started to go inside for cigarettes, he appeared as if out of nowhere.

"God!" I exclaimed, "You scared me to death."

"I'm sorry, Wendy, I didn't mean to."

He was smiling at me. He looked so friendly that I smiled back. I saw that he was wearing the same jeans he'd worn the day before. And then I noticed something else. Rudely, I reached up to his throat, linked my finger through a chain he wore around his neck, and withdrew it from under his shirt, to reveal a round silver pendant. On one side was a star inside a pentagram; on the other side was a sword and the words *Ero tosi*. Immediately I was reminded of Myrna's amulet. And then I remembered that Benjamin had said he knew Myrna.

"Where did you get that?" I asked, releasing it.

"Um, from some guys," he said, carefully and hastily tucking it back into his shirt. I could tell he regretted letting me see it. I felt like I was on the brink of learning something he was reluctant to tell me.

"What guys?"

"Don't think you're ready to hear about them yet," he answered briefly, and turned to go. But I seized him by the arm and made him look at me again.

"Believe me, I'm ready," I assured him irritably. He studied me, glanced around furtively, then pulled me aside, out of the way of the passersby.

"Well, okay, here's the deal. These guys. They're, well, they're not your run of the mill guys. They're sort of different."

"Different?"

"Yeah. Like, well, they gave me this talisman." He indicated the pendant, as if that answered my question. But of course it didn't.

"I know they gave you that, you just *told* me they gave you that," I said. I needed a cigarette real bad. "But who are they? Occultists or something?"

"No, they're more like...I guess you could call them...sorcerers."

My mouth dropped open.

"What are you talking about?" I demanded, and for some reason I was livid. It seemed like everyone knew what was going on but me. "What do you mean, *sorcerers*?"

"Nothing. Forget it," he said, and his eyes were looking past me, anxiously scanning everyone who walked by. I turned around and looked, too, but of course I had no idea what I was looking for, so I turned back to face him again. "Got a cigarette?" he said.

"I'm going in for some," I said, and recalled that we'd had the same conversation the day before. "Wait right here for me, okay?"

He didn't answer. He didn't nod or shake his head. He just kept looking at the people going by. Again, I wondered if he was insane. "Wait right here," I repeated, and went into the Store 24.

I grabbed some cigarettes and headed for the cash register. Absently, I glanced at the tabloids; like I said, I'd been reading them for the series on societal decadence I was doing. And then I nearly fell over when I saw one of the headlines: "Sorcerers spotted near Swan Boats."

I was uncomfortably warm as I picked it up and scanned the story.

"Three tiny old men with long white beards were seen in the Public Garden yesterday performing 'some kind of magic spells,' our witness claimed. According to Delores White of Dorchester, 'They were very short, probably about as tall as a two year old.' She denied that they were midgets masquerading, because their eyes 'were a very strange, very bright blue.' White went on to say that as soon as the sorcerers saw her, they ran away. 'We tried to stop them,' she told this reporter, 'but they moved too fast. It was as if they were flying or something.'"

There was a picture - an artist's rendition - and I was astounded when I saw that the drawing was almost identical to the men I'd seen in my dream the night before. I was so spooked that goose bumps crawled all the way up my arms to my neck. For a minute I didn't move at all, I just stood there,

feeling my heart thud against my ribs and staring at the picture.
All the terror of the night before came back to me. "Does this
mean it wasn't just a dream?" I muttered. "Were there
sorcerers in my room last night?"

"Buying that paper or what?" the guy behind the counter
demanded. I looked up and saw that it was the owner,
Mohammed. He was grinning at me. I buy cigarettes from
him so often that we've become pretty good friends. He
always wants to know if I've written him into my book.

"Um, yeah, I guess so." I didn't feel like joking with him
or telling him that my book would probably never see the light
of day. I put the paper and the cigarettes on the counter.
Mohammed rang up the total and relayed it to me. He was
chewing gum, and placidly blew a pale pink bubble while he
waited for me to hand over the appropriate amount of money.
However, I discovered that I didn't have quite enough - all I
had was change. I could buy either the cigarettes or the paper,
but not both. Hot with embarrassment, I said as casually as I
could, "Uh, guess I won't get the cigarettes after all. Trying
to cut down."

"That's good, you smoke too much," Mohammed beamed,
revising the tally and reaching out his hand for it. I gave him
a couple of quarters and hurried out to show the paper to
Benjamin. But to my disappointment, he wasn't anywhere in
sight. I felt abandoned and betrayed, and spent several seconds
looking up and down the street, even though I knew he'd gone.
I walked a few paces, then dropped onto a bench along the side
of the street and read the story again. Funny that Delores
White of Dorchester should use the word "sorcerer." I mean,
she said they performed magic - why hadn't she called them
magicians? I thought again about the book Scott Bedford had
offered to loan me. Just what the hell was going on, anyway?

64

"Hey, Wendy," a voice beside me said suddenly. With a startled gasp, I turned around to see David approaching. He wasn't really smiling, but at least he was a more or less familiar face, and I was glad to see him.

"David! Have a seat." I patted the bench invitingly, and he obligingly sat, right on some initials and a plea to "Eat The Rich."

"Yeah, okay," he said. I could tell he was puzzled by my obvious pleasure. He was probably thinking, Wait a second. I spent the night with her last night, then left without a word this morning. How come she's not pissed? and he regarded me with a quizzical near smile. As for me, I was grinning broadly. It would be getting dark soon, and I just realized that I could probably invite David to stay over again. That way I wouldn't have to be alone. Scott Bedford's sweet face popped into my mind, but I pushed it aside. This has nothing to do with him, I thought.

"Look at this."

I handed him the paper, and pointed to the headline about the sorcerers. I was feeling a little sheepish, but I didn't care. He frowned.

"Don't tell me you read this shit."

"I don't! I mean, I'm just using it as a resource for my piece about-"

"Sorcerers?" he interrupted.

"Well, yeah."

"Wendy, you don't believe that someone actually saw sorcerers here in Boston. Do you?"

"But there's a picture," I said weakly. He barely glanced at it. "What I mean is, it sounds so stupid. Why would someone make up a story like that? Why would someone say they saw sorcerers if it wasn't true?"

"To see their name in print. Wendy! What the hell is wrong with you?"

I debated whether or not to tell him there'd been sorcerers in my bedroom last night, and decided it might sound a teensy bit silly.

"Nothing. I guess the drawing just triggered a childhood fear, or something." I forced myself to shrug. David nodded absently, having already lost interest in the discussion.

"Listen, Wendy," he said.

"What."

"I need to talk to you."

"Good. I need to talk to you, too."

We both rose. I gave him what I hoped was a seductive smile. For the first time I noticed how tall he was. I felt very safe with him. I even took his hand as we started to walk.

"You first," I said.

"Well, the thing is...about last night..."

"Yes?"

"Well, I'm really sorry about that. I shouldn't have stayed with you. I mean, we don't even know each other. And I, well, I already have a girlfriend. I'm really sorry."

As he tactlessly wriggled his hand out of mine, I stopped walking and stared up at him, full of dismay. That meant I'd have to spend the night in my apartment alone! I felt myself break into a sweat. David mistook my terror for disappointment, and gently touched my cheek.

"I'm really sorry," he said again. "Maybe if we'd met at another time it could have worked out. But we can still be friends, can't we?"

I just didn't know what to say. I couldn't look at him anymore. I was feeling cowardly and not just a little humiliated. I couldn't remember if a guy had ever refused to spend the night with me before. Wouldn't you just *know* it would happen tonight, of all nights!

"Sure, yeah, friends," I said blandly. He took pity on me.

"Lemme buy you a drink," he said. I nodded, and we walked to Max's without speaking.

We hooked up with some other people at Max's and began to drink in earnest. I kept saying, "Just one more," until I was dizzy and my brain was thumping in my head.

"I really should get going, I have a date with What's her name," David said at one point, and giggled drunkenly. I giggled too, not because I thought it was funny, but just to be polite so that maybe he'd spend the night with me after all.

But at midnight he held up his hand and said, "That's it. I really have to go now."

"Just one more," I begged.

"M'sorry, no," he said, shaking his head with exaggerated sweeps back and forth. I envied his inebriation. It was useless to argue with him. I led him out, pointed him in the right direction, and watched him stagger down the street. He rounded a corner, and I was alone.

"What should I do, I can't go home!" I whimpered. I looked up and down the street, hoping someone would come along and rescue me. But of course no one did. I reached into my purse for a cigarette before I remembered that I didn't have any. My fingers came upon something else, which I pulled out. "What's this," I murmured, holding it up to the street light. With a very pleasant start I realized it was the envelope that bore Scott Bedford's address. I felt my face light up.

"I'll go tell Scott Bedford everything!" I said out loud, "He'll know what to do!"

Tucking the envelope back into my purse, I hurried up the street.

CHAPTER TWO

Like me, Scott lived in a brownstone building in the Back Bay area. But his place was a little closer to the heart of the city, and it had recently been renovated. I saw that he occupied the first floor of a three story house, the way I did. Almost delirious with expectation, I knocked hard on the door. I never wear a watch, so I had no idea what time it was. This occurred to me when I heard a very sleepy voice say, "Who is it."

"Scott? It's Wendy. We met at the bookstore a little while ago." Suddenly I was acutely uncomfortable. It was probably going on 1:00 a.m. What was I going to tell him? That there were sorcerers in my apartment?

There was a long pause. I started to sweat. Then he asked what I wanted. I couldn't tell if he was annoyed or not. I figured he'd be intrigued initially; then later, when he found out why I was there, he'd probably be pissed. I've learned that if there's one thing men hate, it's getting roused from a deep sleep for reasons other than having sex.

"I hate to bother you, but can I come in?"

There was another silence. A real long one. I shiver ran through me. I wondered what I'd do if he turned me away. Maybe I could wander the streets until the sun came up. But how safe would that be? Scott had to let me come in, he just had to.

"Okay, hold on a second, Wendy."

I fell against the door, weak with relief. A second later it opened, and I nearly fell inside. There stood Scott, wearing nothing but a pair of gym shorts. White with black piping, and a college logo on the right thigh. I saw that his chest was broad but not overly muscular, and had just the right amount of hair on it. I forced myself to face him, desperate to determine if he was wishing he'd never met me. I was glad to see he was smiling a little, amicably curious.

"Come on in."

I walked in and he shut the door behind me. I looked around. His apartment was bigger than mine, but still pretty small. His wallpaper, kelly green fleur-de-lis on an ivory background, looked new. In the corner sat a stack of expensive stereo components. The walls were bare except for a poster of Einstein that had the caption, "The man who regards his own life and that of his fellow creatures as meaningless is not merely unhappy but hardly fit for life." He had no furniture, no couch or anything. And there were books everywhere. They filled bookcases, and they were piled high on the floor. I was amazed.

"It looks just like your store in here," I said.

"I read a lot," he affirmed unnecessarily. "So, what's up."

"Sorry to wake you," I said slowly. I wasn't quite ready to tell him why I was there yet. I kept looking around, and I also tried to get a look into what I assumed was the bedroom. What if there was another woman in there? What if I'd interrupted-

"That's okay," he said, "I wasn't quite asleep yet."

Why don't you just say it, I thought angrily, Why don't

you just say you were in your room having sex with some cheap-

"Coffee?"

I nodded gratefully. He wasn't going to kick me out right away, and he wasn't going to force me to tell him why I was there until I was ready. He went into his kitchen and I cocked my ear in the direction of the bedroom to see if I could detect someone breathing. I couldn't. So I said brightly, "Hey, finish that book yet? The one about the sorcerers?"

"About ten minutes ago," he said, emerging from the kitchen with an amused smile on his face. "That why you came over? To borrow the book?"

"Well, I mean, you said I could," I defended myself. I could tell my face was pink, and I hated that.

"That's right, I did," he said, still smiling. Something went DING! in the kitchen. He disappeared, and returned a moment later with two steaming mugs, both of which said "Be The Best You Can Be."

"Decaf," he said, handing me one. "If I have caffeine this late I'll be up all night..." His voice trailed off. I could tell he was wondering if he was going to be up all night anyway. I accepted the mug with a nod of thanks, sipped it, then sighed and looked around some more. I just couldn't decide how to begin.

"Sure is nice of you to let me borrow that book," I said. "I mean, shit! You don't even know me, and yet you're willing to-"

"Hey, Wendy, are you going to tell me what you want?"

"I'm getting to that," I said.

"Okay."

I took another sip of coffee. Usually I hate decaf, but at that moment it tasted pretty good. I considered switching to it. Maybe I'd be less jumpy.

"About the book, the one about the sorcerers..."

"Yes?"

"Well, do you believe that those sorcerers really existed?"

"Like I told you before, I'm not sure if I believe it or not. It's kind of like the way I feel about UFO's. I want to believe in them, I want to believe there's life on other planets."

"Uh huh."

"But I don't know for sure. And anyway, whether or not those sorcerers existed isn't really the point of the book. The author, Dr. Holdsworth, emphasizes the need to believe we can all do magic. You don't need to be a sorcerer."

"Oh."

Scott suggested we sit at the kitchen table, which we did, and he sipped his coffee patiently. I couldn't believe how nice he was being about having me arrive at 1:00 in the morning and not tell him why.

"Here goes," I said.

"Okay."

"Well, some really strange things have been happening to me lately, and you're the only person I know who might understand."

We both waited. I was hoping I'd be able to continue, but I was having trouble pulling my thoughts together. For several seconds we sat there, sipping decaf coffee and not talking. Then I finally launched into the story, beginning with my conversations with Myrna and Benjamin, and including my dream about sorcerers, and concluding with the headline I'd read earlier that evening. He listened attentively, nodding now and then, but not saying anything until I mentioned the newspaper. Then he actually laughed.

"That's really amazing," he said, "know why?"

71

I already knew why it was amazing, but I said, "Why" anyway.

"Well because Delores White, the woman they interviewed, is a good friend of mine. In fact, I was talking to her earlier this evening. She was telling me about the sorcerers she saw near the Swan Boats."

"Do you believe her?"

"Of course I do. I've known her for years. She's never lied to me before. In fact, I'm going over to see her tomorrow. Want to come along?"

It was like a date! I nodded eagerly. But then right away I began to wonder just how close he and Delores were. Were they lovers? Were they engaged? I tried to hide my sudden frown.

"In the meantime," he went on, "are you afraid to go back to your place?"

I nodded again. What was he going to suggest? I concentrated on looking as helpless as I could.

"Want to crash here? I have a sleeping bag I can use. You can have the bed."

"I wouldn't dream of kicking you out of your bed!" I cried in a voice shrill with excitement. But he shook his head easily.

"I don't mind a bit. Just let me go in and straighten up a bit."

"You don't have to do that," I said, but I let him do it anyway. Good. That meant there was no one in there. I waited several seconds, then rudely followed him in.

"It's really a mess," he apologized. He was hastily trying to make the bed, which seemed a little silly to me. I looked around. There were stacks and stacks of books. The only place I'd ever seen more was in the Boston Public Library.

"At least there's no place for your sorcerers to hide in here, and there's no way they can get in without knocking something over."

I tried to see if he was making fun of me. I didn't think he was, because he was grinning guilelessly. He reminded me of one of those huge dogs that are always glad to see you. Not the sniff your crotch kind, but the ones who insist on standing in front of you and impeding your movement until you've patted them and complimented them. I realized that I was finally starting to relax. Scott had a very comforting effect on me. Not only that, he had an appealing, drowsy look in his eyes that was driving me straight out of my mind.

"I sure appreciate this," I said.

"Don't mention it. Let me know if you need anything, or if you get scared during the night. I'll be right in the next room. Okay?"

I nodded. I wanted to thank him again, but I was so grateful that I felt shy. So I just stood there, nodding and not thanking him and trying not to stare at him.

"Goodnight, Wendy."

"Goodnight."

With a final smile, he went out, shutting the door gently behind him. I considered asking him to leave it open, but then I figured that if the sorcerers came in through the living room, they'd have to open the door, and I'd hear them and wake up. On the other hand, hadn't my door been closed the other night? I shuddered. "I have to think about something else," I muttered. The light was still on - and believe me, it was going to stay on - and I looked around the room some more. The stacks of books were too overwhelming to even consider going through, so I made my way over to his desk and picked up a couple of photographs that were lying there. I half expected them to be pictures of books, but they weren't. They were pictures of Scott and miscellaneous people, none of whom, naturally, were familiar to me. I studied all the women in the photos, trying to determine if any of them seemed to be his girlfriend. Then, when I couldn't figure that out, I put them back and looked around some more. Tucked in the blotter were a couple of bills that I was tempted to go through. If there was a number on the phone bill that he called often, that would probably mean that he had a girlfriend somewhere. But I didn't look at them; not out of any sense of principles, but because I was afraid he'd come in and catch me.

There wasn't anything else to look at. I was afraid to look in the closet. So I pulled off my dress, laid it across a set of encyclopedias, and crawled into bed. The pillow smelled nice and masculine, not sweaty or anything, but rich with the fragrance I noticed clinging to Scott. I wrapped my arms around it and inhaled deeply. I assumed I'd have trouble falling asleep, but I didn't, I dropped off right away.

Several hours later I woke up suddenly. I sat up too scared to even tremble. The room was very dark, and black, menacing shadows leered at me from every side. I was terrified. At first I didn't know where I was, but after several tense seconds, I remembered that I was in Scott's apartment. For a while I sat there, perfectly still, clutching that nice smelling pillow, waiting for my eyes to become accustomed to the darkness, and listening as hard as I could. From the other room, I could hear Scott's deep breathing. I took courage in that, and leaned over and turned on the light. My eyes scanned the room. I didn't see any sorcerers. Everything looked exactly the same as when I'd gone to bed. I let out a giant breath and tried to calm down, but I couldn't. I mean, you can't experience that much fright, then simply relax because your fear was unfounded. Not only that, I recalled that I'd specifically left the light ON.

"The sorcerers must have come in and shut it off!" I said quietly. "But why?"

I debated whether or not to go wake up Scott. After all, he said I could if I wanted to. And I sure wanted to. But I didn't want him to think I was a coward. But...I *was* a coward, wasn't I. I just didn't know what to do. I wound up lying there, thinking about everything and wishing I had a cigarette, until dawn. For some reason I felt that as soon as the sun came up, I'd be safe. And sure enough, as soon as it began to grow light out, I fell sound asleep.

A knock on the door woke me a few hours later. I'd been dreaming I was back at home, and the person at the door was my mother. So I sleepily granted permission to enter.

The door opened and Scott poked his head in. Was I surprised! I sat up, hastily covered myself with the sheet, and tried to recover.

"Sorry," he said, politely averting his eyes.

"That's okay. What time is it?"

"About 10:00. I told Delores I'd be over at noon. How did you sleep?"

I rubbed my eyes and tired to remember. Then it came back to me and I said, "Scott! The sorcerers were in here last night!"

The expression on his face didn't change. He looked at me for a second, then said, "They were?"

"Yes! They were here and they turned off the light! I left it on, but when I woke up it was off and I was so-"

Scott clapped his hand over his mouth, and said, "Wendy, I'm sorry! I turned off the light. It was shining out from under the door right in my eyes. It was keeping me awake. So I snuck in and turned it off. I'm really sorry. You were asleep and I didn't think you'd notice."

I sat back, half relieved and half disappointed. Well that explains that, I thought. Then I tried to picture the way I must have looked when Scott snuck in. Had I been safely under the sheet, or had parts of me been exposed? Suddenly I was too embarrassed to meet his eyes.

"Other than that, how did you sleep," he asked, and I could tell without looking at him that he was smiling.

"Fine," I lied.

"Need to take a shower before we go or anything? You want breakfast?"

I yawned enormously, then shook my head.

"No, thanks. I'll just wash my face and get dressed. I haven't had breakfast in years. Don't worry about me, you do whatever you'd do if I wasn't here."

"Okay, I'll jump in the shower, then. I won't be long. Will you be okay?"

I nodded. His concern was very gratifying. He nodded too, took a moment to dig out another pair of gym shorts from his dresser, then left. As soon as I heard the bathroom door shut, I got up, climbed back into my dress, and peeked fearlessly into the closet. I recognized a lot of the shirts there because I'd seen him wear them at the bookstore. I didn't see any sorcerers. Quietly closing the door, I went into the kitchen to make coffee. While it perked, I washed my face in the kitchen sink. By the time Scott emerged smelling pleasantly of shampoo and warm, moist air, I was completely refreshed and ready to go.

CHAPTER THREE

I assumed we'd take the subway to get to Delores' house, but Scott surprised me by owning a car. I was impressed. No one in my crowd had one. None of us even knew how to drive. Living in the city, we all depended on public transportation. But Scott said he needed a car to visit his parents in Vermont every couple of months.

"Beautiful countryside, Vermont," I remarked. I was eager to get on his good side so that he'd keep being sweet to me. I'd never actually been to Vermont, but I'd seen pictures, and it looked really pretty. Lots of cows. The air was supposed to be nice and fresh up there, too. "That where you grew up?"

He nodded, and to my surprise, began to speak at length about his home state. I could tell he took real pride in it as he described huge granite quarries, bizarre grave stones in a cemetery near him, and a museum filled with stuffed birds.

"Huh," I said.

"You should see it. You like museums?"

I said I loved museums and that I'd love to see that one, and I hoped he wouldn't notice that I was gushing. When he fell silent, I made up a little fantasy about him taking me to Vermont to meet his parents. They'd say approvingly, "We

77

really like her, Scott," and he'd pull me close and say, "I'm glad to hear that, because I'm going to spend the rest of my life with her."

Before I knew it, Scott was pulling over in front of a large, grey house with a big yard. I saw that the mailbox actually wasn't a box at all, but a hollow goose that had a wing instead of a flag, with the name "White" painted on it. Scott told me that Delores was a nurse, and that she lived alone after having been divorced from a guy who made her eat food she didn't like. I said, "Oh" and followed him up the front steps. I still didn't know what Scott's relationship with her was, I didn't know if they were just friends, or what, and I was dying to find out.

He opened the door without knocking, and preceded me in, calling, "Delores?"

We heard someone say, "Scott? That you?" and then we heard footsteps hurrying our way. A moment later, Delores appeared. My first impression was that she was very petite, with thick, dark, artificially curly hair, and beautiful eyes that were accentuated by professionally applied eye liner. She wore a pair of crisp white slacks that showed off her nice, trim figure. I thought she was very pretty, but more than that, I was struck by the warmth in her expression. I glared at Scott as he kissed her and hugged her tightly. Then he pulled away and introduced us.

"Nice to meet you, Wendy," Delores said, and her voice was friendly.

"Nice to meet you," I mumbled.

"Wendy read about your experience in the paper, and when I told her I knew you, she wanted to meet you. That okay?"

I thought I detected a tiny frown on Delores' face.

"It really happened," she said.

"I believe you," I said, surprised by her defensive tone. "Some pretty weird things have been happening to me, too."

When I said that, her broad smile returned, and she said she'd like to hear all about it. Linking her arm through Scott's, she said we were just in time for lunch.

Over multicolored pasta salad, Delores told us exactly what she'd seen.

"There were three of them. They were tiny, with white beards and very blue eyes."

Scott and I nodded. All of this had been in the article.

"You said they were performing magic," I prompted her. Delores chewed her pasta salad slowly. It was full of orange, green, and beige twists, and she'd put in some cheddar cheese, too, which was a nice touch. "What kind of magic?"

"Well, I didn't tell the reporter this, because it sounds too crazy. I'll understand if you don't believe me, but I swear to you, it really happened."

"What," Scott and I said together.

"Well, I saw the sorcerers talking to some squirrels."

"What?" said Scott.

"Honest! These sorcerers were carrying on some kind of conversation with some squirrels. And the squirrels - there were probably four or five of them - were sitting in a half circle, listening very carefully, and sometimes they'd kind of answer in their little squirrel voices. I'M TELLING THE TRUTH," she insisted when she saw the look on our faces. "They were communicating with the squirrels. And after a minute, the squirrels stood on their hind legs and did a little dance-"

"The squirrels did a little dance?" Scott interrupted.

"I know it sounds bizarre, but I'm telling you, it happened. See why I didn't tell the reporter any of this?"

Scott and I said we sure did.

"So the squirrels did this little dance-"

"Did the sorcerers dance, too?" I wanted to know. I honest to God wasn't making fun of her, but she looked offended as she shook her head.

"No, they just smiled. They had very sweet smiles, like three wise old men. They were really darling."

"So then what," Scott pressed. I could tell he was getting a little impatient. I was still trying to figure out if he was in love with Delores or not. I was beginning to think not, because they're weren't holding hands or gazing into each other's eyes or anything. Scott was eating his pasta salad zealously, and didn't even care that he had a little bit of mayonnaise on his chin.

"Well, so then the sorcerers - and this part is really hard to believe..." She paused. Scott sent me a look that said "*This* part is?" I shrugged and she went on, "Well, one of the sorcerers reached into his pocket, and pulled out a little vial of powder, and he sprinkled some of it on one of the squirrels."

We waited for her to continue, but she didn't until Scott said, "Yes?" and then she took a deep breath and said, "Well at first nothing happened. But then the squirrel flew into a tree."

"What do you mean," Scott said.

"I mean," Delores said, and her eyes challenged us to doubt her, "that the squirrel flew into a tree. It stood up and gave a little leap, and flew ten or twelve feet, and landed on a high branch. Honest."

Scott and I were silent. He'd even stopped eating. We

didn't dare look at each other. I think we might have giggled.

"You sure?" Scott asked eventually.

Delores nodded. "The squirrel flew. It stood up and took off, just like a bird. It didn't even need to run first, it just burst into flight."

"How about that," I said when Scott didn't comment. It sounded silly to me, but I knew that when I told Delores the sorcerers had scared me right out of my apartment, she'd probably fall down laughing. Meanwhile, Scott was staring so hard at poor Delores that she became uncomfortable and concentrated on stabbing an orange twist lengthwise with her fork.

"I believe you," he announced finally. "You wouldn't make up something like this."

She was visibly relieved. She even reached over and squeezed his hand. But he'd resumed eating his pasta salad and didn't seem to notice.

"Well, so what should we do now?" I wanted to know. "Should we go look for them?"

"Maybe they'll come to you," Scott said. "After all, they were in your apartment the other night."

"They were?" Delores looked skeptical, and I thought, It's only fair. In answer to her question, I shrugged as if to say, "Well, sort of," and then we both looked at Scott. Briefly, he recounted my recent experiences to her. She listened graciously, without laughing, then said, "Well, so do you really think they'll come back?"

"I don't know."

No one said anything for a second. Then I said I'd noticed their strange eyes, too, and Delores and I discussed them for a few minutes, how tiny they were, and so on. All the while, Scott was silent. And then all of a sudden he pounded his fist on the table, startling us both so much that we gasped.

"What!" we said together.

"Why didn't I think of this before?" he exclaimed. Delores and I said, "What" again, and he said, "I mean, it's so obvious!"

"Scott," said Delores, "*What* is so obvious?"

"We'll contact Dr. Holdsworth! He'll know what to do."

"The guy who wrote the book about sorcerers? I asked, and when he nodded, I said, "That's a good idea. But how will we find him?"

"Well, he lives in Boston. Let's try looking him up in the phone book," Scott answered. "I mean, it's not like he's famous and needs to have an unlisted number. Right?"

Delores and I said "Right," and she fetched her phone book. Scott flipped through it to the H's. Sure enough, in among the Holdsworths we found a Mason living in Cambridge.

"That's got to be him," Scott said excitedly. "Let's go."

So we jumped into his car and headed for Cambridge. It was another hot day, and as we drove past the shops on Mass Ave, I saw that everyone was dressed in shorts and tank tops. For all its antiquity, a lot of the residents of Cambridge are very avant garde. I couldn't help staring at some of the hair styles, which were either an unusual color, or two unusual colors, or shaved on one side, or standing up very high. I started to say something about it to Scott, but he had such a pleasant smile on his face that I figured it would never occur to him to make fun of someone who was different. So I kept quiet.

Pretty soon we pulled up to a brownstone. Scott said he couldn't believe his luck, that there was a parking space right out in front.

"Not that I would have minded the walk," he said, shutting off the engine and grinning at me, "but to be able to park even on the same block as where you're going is really a kick."

Delores, who also had a car, said she knew exactly what he meant. I said I couldn't imagine what it would be like to drive in the city, and we all got out and walked up the porch of the brownstone building Dr. Holdsworth occupied. Ivy crawled up the railing and framed the front door. There was a deep red Japanese Maple in the yard that obscured most of the front window. I wondered what it would be like to start each day by looking out your window and seeing nothing but red.

Scott knocked on the door, and we waited hopefully.

"Guess he's not home," Delores said after a minute. Scott knocked again, looking so disappointed that I quickly assured them that any writer worth his salt is home all day, every day, writing. Excluding me, of course, but I had a good excuse - there were sorcerers at my home.

Anyway, there was no response to the second knock, and we were about to give up when suddenly I saw a little movement in what I could see of the front window. It looked to me like the shade had moved a tiny bit.

"Someone *is* inside," I hissed. Scott said, "Yeah" because he'd seen the shade move, too, and called out Dr. Holdsworth's name very sternly. We waited some more. And finally we heard a voice say warily,

"Who are you. What do you want."

Delores and I turned to Scott. This had been his idea - it was up to him to take charge.

"Dr. Holdsworth, we need to talk to you. It's very

important."

There was no answer at first. Then we heard the voice say, "Why. Who are you."

"We need to talk to you about your book," Scott said, glancing at me with a doubtful frown; like, what was wrong with this guy? "We need your advice about something."

Finally the door opened a crack. We couldn't see in. All we could see was one suspicious, frightened eye.

"Please let us in," Scott said, "or come out here and talk to us."

"No, I can't do that. Tell me exactly who you are and what you want."

We exchanged helpless looks. How come things never work out the way you expect them to? I had looked forward to chatting with an old white haired professor, sipping tea and listening to clocks tick away the hours. Instead we were peering through this one inch of visibility at an eye, begging for information. Scott heaved a gigantic sigh, then plunged into an explanation, which sounded haphazard and unlikely. I tried to help out, embellishing on a few of the facts, but it still sounded foolish. By the time we reached the end, we'd lost hope.

"Sorry to have bothered you," Scott mumbled when Dr. Holdsworth made no immediate response. We began to move slowly and sheepishly off the porch. But then all of a sudden the door flew open and I was pulled roughly inside. I grabbed Scott, and he grabbed Delores, and SLAM! went the door behind us. We found ourselves in a darkened room that stank of dampness and spoiled food.

Dr. Holdsworth said in a desperate, urgent voice, "Tell me everything again. Slower and with more details."

I felt, rather than saw, Scott turn to me. Then he began

84

the story again. He said he'd enjoyed *Creating The Magic Within Yourself*, and that I'd showed up unexpectedly at his door claiming to have seen the sorcerers in my room, and that Delores had seen the sorcerers performing magic in the Public Gardens, and that we needed to know just what the hell was going on.

As I listened to Scott hurry through the explanation, my eyes gradually adjusted to the darkness. I studied Dr. Holdsworth curiously. I saw that he was in his mid fifties, wearing glasses that rode low on his nose. He had steel grey hair and a coarse grey moustache that twitched a lot. As he listened to Scott, he kept biting his lip and peeking from time to time out the window. Each time he lifted the shade, a stream of light snuck in, and I saw he was actually trembling. I couldn't wait to find out what was going on.

Finally Scott came to the end, and stared expectantly at Dr. Holdsworth. We were astonished to hear him groan and sink his face into his hands.

"What is it? What's wrong?" I demanded. He looked up, and we saw that his eyes were full of fear.

"We're all in very grave danger," he said.

CHAPTER FOUR

For several seconds we just stared with mouths open, trying to decide if we'd heard him correctly. Very Grave Danger. What did that mean?

"Would you mind explaining yourself," Scott said. We weren't really scared. Just surprised. Dr. Holdsworth sighed again, and dropped his hands into his lap. He looked defeated, as if he'd been fighting in a war all month.

"Some guys are after me," he said. " Once they discover that you know me, they'll be after you, too."

"Great," I said. "How come?"

"Because I have something they want. Something they figure they can make a fortune from. In fact, they could even rule the world with it."

"What," asked Scott, but he obviously wasn't expecting to be told. And sure enough, Dr. Holdsworth shook his head.

"Just some esoteric knowledge that they'd kill me for," he said.

"Isn't that always the way," I said, glancing at Scott as if to say, "Well, what now?" He shrugged. I looked back at Dr. Holdsworth and said, "Does this knowledge have anything to do with the sorcerers in Boston? Because if it does, maybe we can all put our heads together, find the sorcerers, and get

86

them to help you."

"You're Wendy Jenkins, are you not?" he asked suddenly. We hadn't told him our names yet, but by now I was getting used to my notoriety, so I just nodded.

"Well, Wendy," he said, "Make no mistake about this. There are no sorcerers in Boston. The last sorcerer in the Great Line died at least a thousand years ago."

Scott and Delores and I all looked at him and then at one another. We were at a loss. We knew for a fact that at least three sorcerers were still around, and here we were, talking to an expert on sorcerers who glibly denied the possibility of their existence. He was obviously lying. But why?

"Look," I said, "Suppose you tell us everything you know about sorcerers. For example, if any were still living, how would we go about finding them?"

Dr. Holdsworth leapt suddenly to his feet and exploded, "Young lady, I told you, there are no sorcerers alive today! Now get out of here!"

We all took a couple of steps back. God, he was weird.

"Calm down," Delores advised in a very warm, tender voice. It seemed to soothe Dr. Holdsworth, who settled back into his chair, and once again sank his face into his hands.

"Just leave me alone," he muttered.

For a solid minute we all stood there, staring at him and at each other, and not saying a word. Then Scott said firmly, "We're not afraid of those guys who are after you. I mean, these are the nineties. People don't get rubbed out by mobsters for withholding information anymore. Right?"

"Wrong," said Dr. Holdsworth. "You don't know these guys." There was a tone of resignation in his voice that finally began to unnerve us just a bit.

"Why don't you tell us about them," Delores urged in

her sweet, gentle voice. She even knelt at Dr. Holdsworth's feet, despite the fact that the floor was filthy and she was wearing crisp, white, linen slacks. I couldn't help admiring her. She was so comforting, like a mother when you're little and you have the flu. I mean, it never would have occurred to me to kneel at his feet. As for Dr. Holdsworth, he was regarding her with delight and surprise.

"I'm afraid to," he admitted. "I'm afraid for you. They're probably watching us right now. They probably saw you come in. They probably assume you know as much as I do, and-"

"Oh, probably not," I interrupted recklessly. It was the middle of the day, and impossible to be afraid. "You don't have to tell us anything you don't want to, but we know there are three sorcerers here in Boston, and you know it, too, we *know* you know it. So quit bullshitting us."

"How do I know you're not working for them," said Dr. Holdsworth unhappily. I could tell he wanted to trust us, but he was being cautious. Even Delores was suspect. He looked at her apologetically, and she patted his knee.

"We don't even know who "them" are," Scott objected.

"It's for your own good, son," Dr. Holdsworth said with finality. "It's best that you leave now." He rose and Delores did, too.

I looked at Scott and saw that he was devastated. I suddenly recalled how much he'd enjoyed Dr. Holdsworth's book. It must have been a shock for him to see the author looking so frail and frightened.

"You can't expect us to just walk out on you," I said. "It isn't the American way. I mean, we all have to help each other, no matter what the circumstances." That was reminiscent of the piece Scott had submitted to *The No Frills*

Dirt. He still didn't know I'd been assigned to destroy it, and I felt guilty about that, but what could I do? Besides, in the light of all that had happened, his philosophy didn't seem quite so naive and unrealistic anymore. And as soon as I delivered my altruistic speech, Scott looked at me with an approving grin.

"Wendy's right," he said. "If you were in our shoes, you'd want to help us, right?"

"Yes, I suppose I would," Dr. Holdsworth allowed.

"Tell you what, Dr. Holdsworth," Scott said, and he was full of an idea that made him look like a very young boy. "You can stay with me! That way they won't know where to find you."

Dr. Holdsworth looked tempted. But then he shook his head.

"No, that would be putting you into too much danger. I couldn't possibly-"

"Maybe he could stay at my place," I interrupted. "Maybe I could stay someplace else." Honest, I was only thinking of his safety.

"Hey yeah, Wendy can stay with me," Scott said.

"Yes, do that," Delores said. Scott went over to the window and peeked out.

"There's no one out there. I think we should leave right now."

"Let's go!" I cried, and without a moment's hesitation, we all flew out the door and piled into Scott's car.

"Will they break in and go through your papers when they discover you're gone?" Delores asked, a couple of tense minutes later. She was sitting in the back seat with Dr. Holdsworth. I was up front with Scott. We'd torn out of Dr.

Holdsworth's neighborhood, and were speeding over the Harvard Bridge toward my place in the city. I gave Scott brief directions, but he thought he'd like to drive a little while in order to make sure we weren't being followed. With his gaze fixed steadily on the rear view mirror, he was being just like one of the Hardy Boys.

"Anything of importance has been put in a safe place," Dr. Holdsworth answered Delores' question. His fingers clutched his arm rest. Scott was driving pretty fast. I hoped we wouldn't get a speeding ticket - it would undermine the glamour of the scenario.

"That's good. What do you mean, like in a bank?"

Dr. Holdsworth glanced over at her. It was obvious he didn't like her asking so many questions. I think he was growing a little suspicious of her - he was looking at her like he'd just found out she was one of the thug's mistress or something - and didn't answer.

Scott finally decided to drive to my apartment. He found a parking spot along a curb nearby, and we hurried past several buildings until we reached mine. I let us in and closed the door firmly behind me.

"I just need to pack a few things," I told them. They stood in my living room - there was no place to sit - and looked around. Scott said "Okay," and I went into my room. I didn't know how long I'd be staying with Scott, so I shoved all the clothes I could fit into a blue canvas bag that I've had for years and never used. At the last minute I grabbed my diaphragm and put that in the bag, too, just in case. When I returned to the others I found them sitting on my living room floor. They'd helped themselves to a beer, which they were passing around.

"I'm all set to go," I announced, reaching for a sip. "Or

should we stay here for a while?" I passed the beer to Scott.

"Oh, why don't you young people go out and do what you normally would on such a nice day," Dr. Holdsworth suggested. "I haven't been sleeping very well lately, and now that I'm here I'll probably go straight to bed."

I didn't say anything to that. I'd noticed he was looking around my apartment as if he expected to see something. Just what, I didn't know. But his eyes were darting all over. The beer came back to me, but it was empty. I tried to drink from it anyway, then sent it sailing through the doorway of the kitchen, past the refrigerator, and into the garbage. It was a fabulous shot. I looked around with a smug grin, but no one took any notice of me, they were too busy discussing plans.

"I'm working tonight," Scott was saying, and he glanced at his watch.

"Me, too," said Delores.

"I have some writing to do," I said

"Writing?" inquired Dr. Holdsworth. I explained that I was working on a book and he became very interested. For a couple of minutes, we talked about how impossible it is to get yourself published unless you're famous or you've committed a crime or had part of your body amputated or shot off. Dr. Holdsworth told me he'd written a novel, an outline of which he'd submitted to one hundred and twenty-seven publishers, and not one of them even asked to see the complete manuscript. I sympathized, and griped about Elliot's proposal. I expected Dr. Holdsworth to say, "You're right, you can't compromise yourself for some dumb jerk agent," but he didn't. He smiled a kind of sweet, fatherly smile, and said, "You know, Wendy, it's a fine thing to be realistic. But to encourage a grim reality isn't always the best policy."

"What are you saying?" I asked, baffled.

"I'm saying that the only people who read cynical books are cynics. Why bother to give them what they want? Why contribute to such a disdainful community? I mean, what are they doing for us?"

"But I'm not writing my book for the cynics. I'm writing it for me," I objected.

"Are you, Wendy? I wonder."

I frowned. I've always hated it when people say "I wonder" like that, like they don't believe you for a second.

"I don't mean to criticize you," Dr. Holdsworth went on earnestly, "but I'm sick and tired of picking up books that portray the American dream gone awry. No one's saying the country is perfect. But to sit back and complain about our conditions without actually doing anything about them is lazy and ridiculous. Maybe you think you're offering constructive criticism, but really what you're doing is *de*structive. You're completely rejecting the only thing that, ultimately, will pull us through these hard times, and that's a belief in ourselves and our power to change the world. You take that belief away, and we're doomed. It's that simple."

I didn't have any retort. I stood there thinking hard about what he'd said. I wanted to be pissed or snotty or something, but I couldn't be. Dr. Holdsworth had such compassion, which is something I've always admired, but never cultivated in myself. I can't help it, I'm never exposed to it. All the people I hang around with are angry young artists who have failed to make piles of dough off the American public. We're all very bitter. But I wasn't always this way. When I was a little girl, I was happy and optimistic. I knew right from the start that I wanted to be a writer, and I assumed that if I worked hard, I would succeed, and then I'd meet a nice man, and we'd get married. But it just didn't work out that way.

In the ten years since I graduated from college I've finished half a dozen novels, none of which have ever been accepted for publication. You couldn't blame me for being fed up. Still...maybe Dr. Holdsworth had a point. Maybe I had no right to blame the rest of society for my own failure. I heaved a deep, dissatisfied sigh. It's so difficult to assume responsibility for your situation; it's so much easier to tell yourself that the reason you're not rich is because the public is too ignorant to appreciate you!

I suddenly became aware that the others were watching me intently. Feeling a little foolish, I tried to grin and shrug. I met Scott's eyes, and he gave me a warm smile. I wondered if he thought I was cynical, too. I mean, I didn't think I'd done or said anything to give him that impression, but he didn't seem at all surprised, so he must have known. Maybe I just had a kind of The World Sucks ambiance about me. I knew all my friends did. But if Scott realized that, why would he want to hang around with me? Maybe because we were both involved in this sorcerers thing, and he had no choice. I realized that I'd better clean up my act if I wanted him to fall in love with me once we'd rescued Dr. Holdsworth.

"Well," Delores interrupted my thoughts suddenly, "I have to get going. Scott? Will you drive me home?"

"Yeah," Scott said, scrambling to his feet. The others rose, too. "Let me give you my phone number," he said to Dr. Holdsworth, "in case you need to call for any reason."

Dr. Holdsworth nodded gratefully. In the cheerful light of my sunny little apartment, he no longer seemed mysterious. Scott wrote down his number on a napkin, then suggested that Dr. Holdsworth memorize and destroy it so that the thugs wouldn't find it. I thought that was very clever. Dr. Holdsworth nodded and said he'd do just that, and I saw that he was smiling a little.

"Thanks.   I really appreciate all of this," he said awkwardly but sincerely. It gave us all a good feeling to be helping him. We told him to have a good night, and left. On the way out we glanced up and down the street, not really sure who we were looking for, but looking for them just the same. We didn't see anyone suspicious.

"I'm sure he'll be fine," Scott said. So we climbed into his car and drove back to Dorchester.

"Want to come in for a few minutes?" Delores asked, once we'd arrived at her house, but Scott shook his head with mild regret.

"Better not. Wendy and I both have to get to work."

I was glad he'd said that. When you don't have a regular nine to five job, a lot of people assume you don't really work. They say, "What are you doing tomorrow?" and you say, "I'm working," and they say, "Oh! Did you get a job?" I think that's one of the most difficult aspects of being a writer.

Delores asked us to call her if anything exciting happened, and we promised we would. We watched her walk up to her door, and as soon as she was safely in, Scott pulled away from the curb.

"I'm hungry," he said. "Want to grab an early dinner before I go to work?"

I was so overcome by bliss I could only nod.

"Good. We can get to know each other. We really haven't had much of an opportunity to talk. I'd like to hear more about what you write for *The No Frills Dirt.*"

"Uh huh," I said, glancing out the window. Shit! What was I going to tell him?

CHAPTER FIVE

Scott parked his car more or less in the vicinity of his apartment, and from there we headed to a diner I'd been to a couple of times. I was racking my brain, frantically deciding what I was going to tell Scott about myself, when all of a sudden I heard someone call my name. I recognized the voice at once.

"Benjamin!" I greeted him. "Come over here and meet Scott."

"Hey, how's it going," Benjamin murmured, shaking Scott's hand.

Scott nodded and said, "Nice to meet you," and his eyes scanned Benjamin's attire, from those same torn jeans to the t-shirt which bore a faded Peace sign. "Join us for dinner?"

Benjamin glanced at me and I nodded hopefully. Maybe I could keep the focus of the conversation on Benjamin, and not say a word about myself. After a moment, Benjamin said he'd like that very much. He said he hadn't had a decent meal in a long time.

"Let's go," Scott said, and he'd already opened the door so that Benjamin and I could precede him in. We found ourselves a table, ordered a round of beers, and right away

Scott remarked that he'd always enjoyed the music of the sixties. Benjamin smiled, then frowned.

"Yeah, you got a lot of shitty music that's popular now," he said.

"I don't mean that today's music is shitty," Scott protested, "I'm just saying that back in the sixties you had some interesting causes. The Vietnam War, racism, that kind of thing. You had communes and Free Love. Must have been a really beautiful time."

Benjamin didn't answer right away, because the waitress arrived at that moment to take our order. Benjamin and I both ordered burgers and fries. Scott said he'd have a salad. I was a little surprised, because he didn't look as if he needed to watch his weight or anything, but he said he liked to eat at least one salad a day.

As soon as the waitress disappeared, Benjamin said, "Yeah, I got memories from that time I wouldn't trade with for the world. Not like what the kids today have."

"What do you mean?" Scott said.

"Well, I mean kids today don't really care about the world. Why should they? Look at their heroes - they got purple hair and all they want to do is make money. They don't give a shit if their music is good or not. And suddenly every musician has to be an actor, too. I just don't get it."

"But you're forgetting about all the good they've done. There was Live Aid, Farm Aid, Comic Relief. They've raised millions and millions of dollars," Scott said. He seemed intent on convincing Benjamin that today's generation wasn't just a bunch of lazy degenerates.

But Benjamin smirked and flipped his hand and said, "It's all a publicity stunt. You know how popular you can get with fans if you help the needy?"

"What difference does it make, as long as the homeless get a place to live, and the starving get some food," Scott shrugged, and took a long hit off his beer. I was watching him, and I felt like I had a kind of glow on my face. I wondered if he noticed it. I wondered if he wondered if I had a boyfriend.

"The Beatles were a hell of a band," I put in because I hadn't really contributed much.

Scott said, "Yeah," but he wasn't really concentrating on what I'd said. He was still regarding Benjamin with a mild, steady smile. After a few minutes our food arrived. Even though Scott had requested no onions, there were a ton of them on his salad anyway.

"Man, I'd just send that back," Benjamin said as Scott began to carefully pick them out.

"No big deal," Scott said, and honest to God, he wasn't annoyed or anything. When something doesn't come precisely as I ordered it I fly into a real rage. But Scott didn't mind at all. Benjamin and I ate our burgers and fries in silence. And when the check came, Scott paid for the whole thing. Benjamin and I muttered sheepish thanks, but Scott just held up his hand as if to say, "Don't mention it." Then he rose and asked if he could speak to me alone before he left for work.

"Sure," I said. I glanced at Benjamin and he said he'd meet us at the door, and walked off. "What is it."

"Lemme give you this," Scott said, withdrawing a handful of keys from his pocket. He disengaged one and handed it to me. "The key to my place. I didn't want to give it to you in front of Benjamin. If he's been following you like you say, you don't want him to know you're not staying at your apartment anymore."

"Probably knows anyway," I said, taking the key. "It's really creepy the way he knows everything about me."

"We'll keep our eye on him," Scott said, watching me drop the key into my purse, and then placing his hand gently on my back to steer me over to the door. "I should be home at about 11:00. Will you be up?"

"Are you kidding? I never go to bed before 1:00."

"Okay. Well, I'll see you when I get in."

"Okay." I felt cozy making plans to see him when he got home from work. Like we were married or something. "You want me to fix you something to eat?"

"No thanks. I usually eat at work. I'm afraid I don't have as exciting a lifestyle as you, Wendy. I'll probably just watch the news for a couple of minutes and then go right to bed. I have to be up first thing in the morning to open the store."

"Oh." I was kind of disappointed.

"Sorry."

"That's okay, I know how it is when you have a regular job," I said, and my voice sounded kind of snotty. I think I was kind of trying to hurt his feelings a little bit, because I was mad at him for not showing any signs of falling in love with me. But he didn't even notice. He just shrugged and nodded.

We joined Benjamin who was waiting impatiently by the door. Scott shook his hand again and said he'd see us later, then strolled off down the street toward his bookstore. I watched him while Benjamin watched me.

"He your boyfriend?"

"I don't know."

"I like him."

I looked at Benjamin, and I couldn't help smiling.

"Me too," I said.

"Now I need to talk to you."

"What."

Benjamin glanced up and down the street, and then led me over to a doorway of a bank, out of the way of the people who streamed steadily by us. All the while his eyes were darting this way and that. I felt a little nervous and said, "What" again.

"Wendy, you have to be careful. The danger is getting closer."

I thought back on what Dr. Holdsworth had said about us all being in very grave danger.

"Tell me exactly what you're talking about," I said.

"I'm sorry, I can't. I can't tell you anything more than I've already told you. All I can say is, be on your guard. Don't do anything foolish."

"What are you-"

He held up his hand.

"I can't tell you anymore," he repeated. His slate grey eyes gazed into mine. He actually looked scared. And that bothered me even more than his cryptic warning. I began to say something, but he interrupted, "I'm going to watch over you and protect you as much as I can, but you will still have to be careful." And all at once he stepped back onto the sidewalk and walked quickly away. I watched him disappear, then looked around. It was still mostly light out, and with him gone I was no longer frightened.

"To hell with that," I said boldly, "I'm going to the Public Garden to find those sorcerers. Maybe they'll be able to tell me what's going on."

I tried to decide what I'd say to them. They'd recognize me, of course, since they'd been in my room the night before last. I pictured bringing them back to Scott's apartment and staying up all night chatting with them. Scott would be so thrilled to meet three sorcerers that he'd fall in love with me.

On the way I stopped to get cigarettes, and by the time I got to the Public Garden the sky had begun to turn dusky. I looked around for the sorcerers, but I didn't check under bushes or anything, I just stayed on the sidewalk with everyone else who was walking by. And I didn't see any sorcerers anywhere.

"Oh well, you can't say I didn't try," I muttered, and decided to go to Max's.

A sign on the door said "Masquerade Party Tonight," and people were flooding past me. Inside, the lights were turned up and there were festive streamers hanging from the ceiling and helium filled balloons all over. All the waitresses wore platinum blond wigs and were dressed like Marilyn Monroe. The walls had been covered with a mural of Boston's skyline, and even though it was still early in the evening, the place was packed. I knew I'd be safe. So I went in, hoping to run into someone I knew. And sure enough, I wasn't there five minutes before someone took my arm. Relieved, I turned to see who it was. To my shock I found myself staring at someone dressed as a menacing gangster. He wore sunglasses and a hat which covered most of his face, and he had a thin moustache I didn't like the looks of. Roughly, he grabbed my arm and growled that I was to come with him.

"Let me go!" I screamed, struggling to get away. I hit him as hard as I could, and then I kicked him in the shin, just below the kneecap. He let out a howl of pain and released me at once.

"Jesus Christ, Wendy!" I heard him say, and suddenly

his voice sounded familiar. I reached up and took off his sunglasses, and saw that it was Rich.

"Oh my God," I said, cupping my hands over my mouth. "I'm so sorry!"

"Guess I know better than to fuck with you," he said, leaning down to rub his shin.

"I didn't recognize you."

"That's okay. Pretty authentic costume, huh."

"Yeah. Hey, you want to dance?"

"You kidding? I can barely walk. Help me over to my table."

He was limping so badly that I apologized six more times on the way over, but he kept saying it was okay. When we reached his table, he introduced a couple of girls that I didn't recognize. We sat down, and pretty soon they asked me if I wanted to go to the Ladies' room with them to snort some coke. I was a little embarrassed as I shook my head. They would have been shocked to know that I've never taken any kind of drugs at all, I haven't even ever smoked pot, which is supposed to be harmless. But I've always cherished this dream of being a great writer, and I guess I decided early on that it wouldn't be possible if I fucked up my head with drugs. See, a long time ago I knew this kid who could draw better than anyone else in the school. He always planned to be an artist. But he wound up getting involved with this bad crowd who got him hooked on drugs, and one night he tried to stop an oncoming train. His body was so completely mangled that it couldn't be shown at his funeral. So every time someone mentions drugs to me I just make up some excuse to say no. Sometimes I tell people that I'm trying to kick a bad drug addiction, and once I said I'd just brushed my teeth.

Anyway, after I shook my head, they got up and left.

Rich giggled, and to my dismay, went with them. Once again, I was alone. But not for long. As soon as they left, a guy dressed as a rabbit asked me to dance. I thought, What's safer than dancing with a rabbit? and accepted. He had some friends with him, all dressed as forest animals, and I danced with all of them. The next time I looked at a clock, it was 10:30.

"I have to leave," I told them.

"Oh no," said one guy who was dressed as a deer. "We're having so much fun."

"I know, but I still have to go," I said.

"Stay ten more minutes," begged a guy who was dressed like a bird. I shook my head.

"I just can't. I'm sorry."

"At least let us walk you home," said the guy dressed like a rabbit. With Benjamin's warning still ringing in my head, that sounded like a good idea. So I started to nod my head; but then I remembered that I wasn't going home, I was going to Scott's place. All of a sudden, it seemed unwise to take them there. What if they were involved with the guys who were after Dr. Holdsworth? I didn't want them to find Scott and kill him.

"Nah, that's okay, I'll be fine," I said. "Thanks anyway."

I turned to go, but they linked their arms in mine and insisted on escorting me out. And once we were out, they said they couldn't let me walk the streets by myself.

"Just wouldn't be safe," said the bird sternly. The deer and the rabbit concurred. So I decided to lead them to my place, pretend to go inside, and then take off for Scott's as soon as they left.

However, when we arrived, the rabbit asked if they could

come in for a nightcap.

"I'm sorry," I said. "I don't have any liquor in the house."

"How about a soft drink," said the deer.

"Don't have any."

"Got a carrot?" asked the rabbit, and they all laughed.

"No," I said. "I'm sorry. Thanks for walking me home."

They insisted on getting a kiss each, which I granted, but refused to leave until they saw me safely inside. So I said, "Goodnight" again, very quietly, then snuck in. And after a second, all three headed back down the street.

"Thank God," I muttered, "I hope I'm not going to be late."

But just as I started to open the door, a hand seized my arm and a voice in my ear snarled, "Sorry, Wendy, but you're not going anywhere."

PART THREE

PROLOGUE

Humming softly, Miss Greenblatt - a spindly, elderly woman with artificial, burgundy colored hair and glasses shaped like the eyes of a cat - shut off all the lights in the library, switched on the burglar alarm, and closed and locked the door. Then she walked to her car, a gigantic gold 1970 Pontiac that she had for years called "The Old Girl." She started up the engine with a roar. Music from the Swing Era poured out the window Miss Greenblatt opened by pressing a button on her door. Ferociously, the Old Girl swung out of the parking lot at nearly eight miles an hour. She'd no sooner disappeared than three small, wrinkled faces appeared from behind a bush near the door.

"Coast is clear," hissed Puu.

"No shit, man," Bni said. He crawled out, adjusting his tall cap. In accordance with The Great Book, *all sorcerers must wear tall caps, each with a different symbol, depending on the orientation of the sorcerer. Cozlu, Puu, and Bni were what they called Celestial Sorcerers, and so their symbols were all objects in the sky. Bni's cap bore a blazing sun. Puu had a slice of moon on his. On Cozlu's cap was a luminescent star. All three sorcerers wore long robes with rope belts knotted at the waist, and deep pockets filled with amulets and vials.*

"Let's go," Cozlu instructed. With a final covert glance around the parking lot, they went up to the door, murmured a few words in low voices, and vaporized. A moment later, they were inside. Puu turned on the light, and in a flurry of excitement, the three little men began to scamper here and there in pursuit of knowledge. Since they'd arrived to the future, they'd been catching up on all that had happened since their lifetimes. Naturally, most of what they learned was pretty

107

shocking. *They were appalled at the wars which had been fought for no apparent reason other than someone's irrational desire to "rule" the world, and modern man's abhorrent lack of respect for his neighbor.*

Sorcerers are very speedy readers. They also require very little sleep. Cozlu, Bni, and Puu easily made their way through hundreds of books a night. For the most part, they spent hours selecting books about scientific discoveries and American history, taking brief naps in between. Occasionally they would read a novel, too, just to round out their education.

"Man, I'd like to have gone on the road with that groovy cat, Jack Kerouac. Maybe we can do another time travel scene, maybe go back a couple of generations," Bni said. His merry little voice broke through the stillness of the library. Cozlu and Puu exchanged exasperated grimaces.

"Bni, stop reading literature from the fifties and sixties," Cozlu said. "No one talks like that anymore. And no one uses phrases like 'groovy' anymore. Frankly, this new phraseology of yours is getting on my nerves."

"Can I help it if it isn't your bag," Bni mumbled, and fell silent. He'd developed a keen interest in the Beat writers. Cozlu and Puu, on the other hand, enjoyed the works of more gentle poets like Robert Frost.

"Look at all these books about changing one's body shape," Puu remarked in mild, disapproving surprise. "Flatten your tummy, flatten your thighs, flatten your rear. And look at this book about painting your face and coloring your hair. Why are 20th century people so reluctant to look like themselves?"

"Sure has become a strange world, alright," Cozlu sighed.

CHAPTER ONE

Someone turned on a light. I saw Dr. Holdsworth cowering against the wall, looking very small and frightened. A big, tough looking guy with a stubbly chin like Fred Flintstone's held him by the arm. Another guy was holding me. I tried to struggle loose, but couldn't, and gave up. There was a third guy there, too, and he was missing a tooth right in front. Three pairs of tiny, nasty eyes glared; three thick lipped mouths sneered.

"What's going on," I demanded, wishing I hadn't been so hasty in sending away my forest friends.

"We're friends of the doctor here," jeered the one who had Dr. Holdsworth by the arm.

"Let Wendy go. She doesn't know anything," Dr. Holdsworth begged in a scared little voice. "Honest. I didn't tell her anything."

"Nah, we want her to stay with us for a little while," said the one holding me. There was something very barbaric and unrefined about the three of them - like they wouldn't have the sense not to kill me.

"Let me go," I said. I tried to kick my captor in the shin; it had been so effective earlier in the evening. But he twisted my arm so painfully that I stopped.

"We'll let you go, alright," said the third guy, "just as soon as you tell us what we want to know."

"And what would that be?"

"You know damn well we wanna know where the sorcerers are," said the guy who was holding Dr. Holdsworth.

"Sorcerers?" I parroted innocently.

"Yeah, *sorcerers*." The guy holding me twisted my arm again With my free hand I scratched him hard. He said, "Shit!" and released me. I scurried over to Dr. Holdsworth, and tried to pull him away from the guy who had him by the arm.

"Please let her go! I'm telling you, she doesn't know anything!" Dr. Holdsworth wailed again, clutching my arm frantically. I saw that his fingers looked stiff and white, and was suddenly reminded of the way my father's hands look on the dashboard when my mother is driving. Fear completely took over then, and I wondered if I would ever see them again. I hoped they knew I loved them. And my brother, too. Even though I've always told him he's an idiot, I hoped he would understand that I never meant it in a bad way.

"She knows what our faces look like, that's something she knows," the third guy said. "And she knows who else is in on this with you."

"In on what? Dr. Holdsworth, who are these guys?"

"This," Dr. Holdsworth inclined his head toward the guy who was still holding him by the arm, "is Spaulding. That," he nodded toward the guy who'd been holding me, "is Rogers. And that," he indicated the third guy, the guy with the missing tooth, "is Brewer. They're the ones I was telling you about. They're the ones who are after me."

"So you *have* told her everything," said Brewer.

"No, no! I mean, I haven't really," Dr. Holdsworth

110

protested, but it was too late. The three thugs were glaring at me.

"All you want to know is the whereabouts of the sorcerers?" I asked in a voice so calm it surprised even me.

"That's right," said Spaulding. He gave Dr. Holdsworth a cruel shove into the wall.

"Well I'll be glad to show you," I said, taking Dr. Holdsworth's hand and leading him toward the door. "Come on."

"What? Where? Where are we going?" The three of them demanded, surprised and suspicious.

"To find the sorcerers. I know where they hang out," I said. Meanwhile, of course, I was sifting through all my options, none of which seemed likely. Where was I going to lead them?

"Wendy, are you sure you know what you're doing?" Dr. Holdsworth hissed into my ear.

"Of course. I'll take these guys to meet the sorcerers, and then they'll leave us alone," I said. The hell they will, I thought, and a thin film of sweat broke out all over my body. But still I maintained my calm. If I got out of this alive, I was going to feel pretty smug. "Coming?" I asked them.

Swapping dubious frowns, Dr. Holdsworth and the thugs followed me out. I was glad I was ahead of them so they couldn't see my face. I was biting my lip, and my eyes were looking everywhere for somewhere to take them. What place would still be open at this time of night? And then it hit me. Max's.

"Come on, it's this way," I said urgently, and began to hurry. But Rogers reached out and grabbed my arm.

"We're coming, just slow down. Don't do anything to attract anyone's attention," he said in a quiet, menacing voice.

We commenced to walk sedately up the street. All the while I was thinking, What am I going to do when we get there? but tried to keep my expression blank. It seemed we arrived too soon - when we reached the club I was still racking my brain.

"Here we are," I said.

The thugs and Dr. Holdsworth and I stood on the sidewalk for a moment. We could hear the smokey thump of the music inside.

"The sorcerers are in here?" Spaulding asked doubtfully.

"Oh yeah, they're big partiers. You know, there are very few night clubs where they come from. Tonight they're masquerading as the Marx Brothers."

I'd already headed toward the door. Rogers still had me by the arm. Brewer was gripping Dr. Holdsworth. But there were a lot of people walking past us, and I felt safer.

"Okay, now what," Dr. Holdsworth asked me.

"Beats the hell outa me," I answered him, but inside it was too loud for him to hear me. My eyes scanned the crowd. If only I could find someone I knew!

"So where are they?" demanded Rogers. His face was very close to mine, and his breath wasn't pleasant. He tightened his grip on my upper arm, and it hurt worse than the time I got my blood pressure checked.

"They said they'd be here," I said. I had to shout to be heard over the music. Meanwhile, I was looking at every face. Everyone was wearing a mask. I looked around for my forest friends, but didn't see them anywhere. "Just keep your eyes open for Groucho, Harpo, and Chico," I told Rogers. "The sorcerers have a great admiration for American slapstick." Rogers nodded and relayed this information to his pals. They still didn't know if they should believe me or not, but I suppose they decided to assume for the moment that I was telling the truth. Dr. Holdsworth was staring at me. I shrugged. What else could I do?

"Hey, Wendy!"

I spun around and saw a police officer hurrying toward us. I couldn't see him face very well, because he was turning his head to the left and right, apologizing to people as he pushed his way past them. A real impressive gun hung at his side. I tried to remember if I knew any cops, but I didn't think I did. When he reached us, his slate grey eyes met mine, and finally I recognized him. Benjamin. Clean shaven, with his long hair hidden under his cap, all set to save my ass. I was so relieved to see him that I almost laughed.

Instead I wriggled free of Rogers' hold and said, "Officer, these guys are bothering my friend and me. I'm pretty sure they're drunk. They keep asking us where the sorcerers are, whatever that means."

Benjamin leered at the thugs who were standing sheepishly in a semi circle around Dr. Holdsworth and me. Then he grinned an arrogant, authoritative grin.

"Well now," he said slowly, "suppose you gentlemen leave this little lady alone. She's a good friend of mine, and I'd hate to have to shoot you in front of all these nice folks."

Casually, he tapped his gun. Spaulding, Rogers, and Brewer exchanged angrily doubtful glances. They didn't know if Benjamin was really a cop or not. Obviously they couldn't afford to take any chances.

"We're not bothering her, officer," Spaulding said. "She's a good friend of ours, too, and we-"

"Doesn't look that way to me," Benjamin interrupted with a frown and took a step toward Spaulding.

"We're just talking to her," Rogers whined.

"Sounds to me like she wants you to *stop* talking to her.

Now I've been assigned to keep the peace in this place tonight. Anyone disturbs it, they get thrown out. Do I make myself clear?"

The three thugs backed off. Benjamin had made himself pretty clear, alright. Dr. Holdsworth was finally released and I took his hand.

"Thanks!" I said, turning to go. But Brewer grabbed me one final time and said in a nasty voice,

"You win this round, Wendy. But don't forget - we know where to find you, and we're not through with you yet, 'little lady.'"

Benjamin didn't hear what Brewer said, but was enraged that Brewer had spoken to me when he'd just been told to leave me alone. Grabbing him by the shoulder pad of his suit jacket, Benjamin started heading toward the door with him. Spaulding and Rogers had no choice but to follow. They sent us killer looks, and left. But as soon as Benjamin disappeared into the crowd, they came right back in and headed toward us. And they looked madder than ever.

"What should we do now?" Dr. Holdsworth asked. He kept holding his hands over his ears. I guessed he wasn't enjoying the music, even though the song they were playing was vintage Led Zepplin. "They're coming back."

"This way," I said, leading him toward the emergency exit.

"Improper use of the emergency exit is against the law," Dr. Holdsworth objected. "The alarm will go off, and we'll get into trouble."

"Stay here and get killed, then," I said, and yanked open the door. A loud BRRRRRRRR! filled the club. The dj turned off the music, and suddenly everyone was desperate to get out. They probably assumed there was a fire somewhere, and, as a single frightened mob, they headed for the door. Spaulding, Rogers, and Brewer got caught up in the mass coming straight toward them, and were unable to advance more than a couple of steps before they were forced to give up. Dr. Holdsworth and I dashed out the emergency exit and took off down the street. We ran as fast as we could, and by the time we reached Scott's apartment I could barely stand up. My lungs felt like they were going to explode. It was probably time to give up smoking.

We found Scott waiting outside. Guiltily, I recalled that I had his key. He saw us running toward him, knew that something was amiss, and scurried out to meet us, then ran back to wait by his door. I pulled out the key, and all three of us tumbled in and slammed the door behind us.

Dr. Holdsworth and I started to explain, but we were so out of breath that we couldn't string together more than two words in a row.

"Hold on, hold on," Scott said, retrieving a beer from the refrigerator, cracking it open, and handing it to me. I barely tasted it. Dr. Holdsworth was still trying to tell Scott what had happened, and he was sputtering "And they...and they...and they..." and so I took over. I handed him the beer, took a deep breath, and told Scott all that had transpired.

"So Dr. Holdsworth was right - we *are* in very grave danger. These guys are mean."

Scott said, "Shit," and reclaimed the beer.

"What should we do?" Dr. Holdsworth wanted to know. He felt badly, I could tell; but of course he'd warned us. We only had ourselves to blame. But actually, I was feeling very stimulated by all the action. My life is usually pretty uneventful. I could tell that Scott felt the same way, because he wasn't scared at all.

"They follow you here, do you think?" he said.

"I don't think so," I said, "but I didn't think they'd followed us to my place, either. They're pretty sneaky."

"So Benjamin rescued you," Scott said, and as he passed the beer to Dr. Holdsworth, he laughed. I laughed, too. Dr. Holdsworth didn't drink any beer, and he didn't laugh. He just sat, holding the can, not even smiling. It was the first time he'd met Benjamin, and he'd been too frightened to take the time to form an opinion about him.

Scott and I took the beer back, finished it, then opened up another while we tried to come up with a plan. But it's very difficult to take action against something you don't completely understand. We considered going to the police with our information, but we couldn't decide what was the best way to tell them about the sorcerers.

"We're just going to have to take care of this ourselves," I said. Scott chuckled, and as he headed toward the refrigerator for one last beer, a sudden loud pounding on the door startled all three of us.

"Who could that be?" I asked, and I could feel my eyes open wide. Gone was my bravado. There was someone at the door who wanted to come in. Badly. I looked at Scott. He was staring at the door. The person outside pounded again. I scrambled over to Scott's silverware drawer and pulled out the biggest knife I found. Silently, I nodded. Scott took a deep breath and opened the door.

CHAPTER TWO

To our surprise, it was Benjamin who charged into Scott's apartment. His eyes took us all in at once, and then he said breathlessly, "Everyone okay?"

We all heaved gasps of relief and nodded. Scott laughed shakily, took the knife from me, and put it back into the drawer.

"How did you know where we were?" I asked, dismayed. Were we so easy to track down? Did the thugs know where we were, too?

Benjamin glanced at Dr. Holdsworth, and said quietly, "I was told where to find you." Dr. Holdsworth looked startled, but then after a second he nodded solemnly. He and Benjamin apparently understood something that Scott and I didn't.

"Yes, young man, we're fine," Dr. Holdsworth told Benjamin. He extended his hand. "Glad you stopped by - I didn't get a chance to thank you before."

"Don't mention it," Benjamin said briefly, shaking hands with Dr. Holdsworth. Turning to Scott and me, he said to be careful. And then without another word, he slipped back out. We heard the door go CLICK behind him, and then we all sat down again at Scott's kitchen table.

"Dr. Holdsworth," said Scott, "I think you'd better plan

to stay here tonight. Wendy's place isn't safe anymore."

"Thank you very much, I'd appreciate that," Dr. Holdsworth said, clearly relieved.

Scott just nodded thoughtfully. I marveled at his unceasing generosity. I think he'd invite every person in the entire city in if they needed a place to stay. Then it occurred to me that his small apartment was going to be pretty crowded. I was going to suggest that he and I could share the bed so that Dr. Holdsworth could have the whole living room floor to himself, but before I got the chance, Scott said that he had another sleeping bag for me. He said that Dr. Holdsworth could have the bed.

"Thank you both so much," Dr. Holdsworth said. "Goodnight." He disappeared into Scott's room, gently shutting the door behind him. Scott went to a closet and pulled out another sleeping bag.

"Here," he said. "You'll be comfortable in this. You don't mind sleeping on the floor, do you?"

I said I guessed not. I mean, what was my other option, sleeping with Dr. Holdsworth? Scott unrolled and laid out my bag about two feet from his. I wondered if I could move it closer while he slept, so that when he woke up I'd practically be in his arms, and he'd accidentally kiss me and fall madly in love with me.

"I'm going to brush my teeth," Scott said, and went into the bathroom. I listened to hear if he was one of those environmentally minded people who shut off the water while they brush, and sure enough, he was. Then I heard him pee. A second later he reappeared and said, "All yours."

I brushed my teeth and peed, too. As I flushed, I studied my face in the mirror. I thought about Delores' eyes, and how pretty she was with all that make-up. Did Scott prefer women who wore make-up? It seems like men are always saying they like their women "natural," but then they practically fall down whenever some beautiful glamour queen walks by. I saw that my hair was a tangled mess. I recalled that I hadn't showered that morning.

"What a wreck," I muttered. Shutting off the light, I returned to the living room. Scott was leaning on one elbow, reading a book about personal and social transformation in the 1980s. I crawled into my sleeping bag, then carefully tugged my dress off over my head and tossed it on the floor, all the while modestly keeping myself covered. Scott watched with interest.

"Hope you don't mind," I said.

"Not at all," he said, "I'm not wearing anything either."

I pinched my lips together so that I wouldn't gasp or moan, and tried not to think of him lying naked so close to me. I wondered what he was thinking about. Probably the sorcerers. After a moment, I pulled myself together and asked him what he thought our next step should be. He closed his book and set it aside. I saw that he was about three quarters of the way through, and that the cover was kind of beat up. Although I'd never read the book myself, I remembered when it came out, because it had caused a real stir among my friends and me. None of them had read it, either, but we'd all criticized it anyway, because it was supposed to be really optimistic and full of encouraging research on the latent abilities of the human brain and all that stuff. From the looks of Scott's copy, he was making his way through it for the fourth or fifth time.

"Well, assuming we're safe here, which of course we may not be, I think you should make sure that Dr. Holdsworth stays out of sight. If you absolutely have to leave the apartment, I'd suggest you disguise him. Don't ask me how," he added hastily, anticipating my question. "Is there anything you need to do tomorrow?"

"I need to go to my place," I said. Actually, I didn't really have to. I just wanted to check my apartment. After all, it had been full of thugs a little earlier in the evening.

"They're probably watching your place," Scott warned me. "If you go there, they may try to jump you again. Maybe you shouldn't risk it. I don't think it would be safe."

I fell silent. The realization that I shouldn't go to my apartment suddenly made it absolutely essential that I go. Suddenly I was mentally inventorying my stuff, thinking, I need that...I need that...I need that...I need that...

"What do you have to get? More clothes? Make-up? Couldn't you just go shopping instead?"

I just shook my head scornfully. Clothes and make-up? Who did he think he was camping with, Elizabeth Taylor?

"I don't know what to say," he said, trying to swallow a yawn. I frowned, thinking about how, no matter what the circumstances, men are unable to lie in bed without falling asleep, unless they're having sex. "I'd worry about you going there. But if you really have to, let's think of some safe way for you to do it."

We tossed a couple of ideas back and forth, then he drifted off. I didn't blame him; it was late and he had to get up early for work. But it was about two hours before my usual bedtime, and I was left lying there on the floor, wide awake and naked, my bag miles from his. The light was still on, so I just lay there looking at Scott. What a sweet face he had, pink and soft with sleep. I tried to imagine what it would be like to have him make love to me. I wondered if he had any brothers or sisters, if he'd ever been married, or if he was secretly in love with anyone the way I was secretly in love with him. And before I knew it, I'd fallen to sleep, too.

Once again, I woke just before dawn. I sat up, rigid, to listen with that same uncomfortable intensity. The room was in total darkness. Scott must have turned off the light. My breath came faster and faster. It seemed like an hour passed before my eyes became accustomed to the dark. And then I saw, over in the corner, those three pairs of brilliant blue eyes shining at me, sparkling with lively curiosity. The sorcerers! I tried to cry out Scott's name, I tried to wake him so that he could see them, too. But when I opened my mouth, no sound came out at all.

I sat up for real, and several moments passed before I realized it had been another dream. The light was still on. Nearby, Scott snoozed like a newborn. My heart was slamming itself against the inside of my rib cage.

"Shit," I muttered, and wondered if I'd ever be able to sleep through the night ever again. As quietly as I could, I crawled out of the sleeping bag, retrieved my purse from over near the door, and began digging through it for cigarettes. The pack was nearly empty. Almost dizzy with anticipation, I lit one and took a long, unsteady drag. But for some reason, it didn't taste as good as I expected it to. I took it back to my bag and smoked it out anyway, thinking about the sorcerers and watching Scott sleep, until the sun came up. Then I finally dozed off.

When I woke up several hours later, Scott was gone. On the floor was the shirt he'd worn the day before. I reached out and brought it into the sleeping bag with me. It smelled strongly of him - his shampoo, his deodorant, his laundry detergent. Wrapping my arms around it, I luxuriated in the fragrance and pretended for a few minutes that he was in the sleeping bag with me. Then I got up, put it on, and began rummaging through the refrigerator for something that Dr. Holdsworth and I could have for breakfast. There were eggs, but no bacon. I peeled and ate an orange while I dropped a couple of slices of bread - whole wheat - into the toaster. All the while I was making as much noise as I could, hoping to wake Dr. Holdsworth. But the door to his room remained shut. I thought that was kind of funny, because usually when you're old you don't need that much sleep and you automatically get up real early. But maybe he'd had trouble sleeping the night before. I had eggs and toast, and made myself a cup of coffee. I was cleaning up the kitchen when all of a sudden the front door opened and in walked Dr. Holdsworth! Was I surprised! Apparently he'd been out all morning.

"Hello, Wendy," he greeted me cheerfully.

"Where have you been?" I demanded.

"Out."

"What do you mean, *out*? It isn't safe for you to leave here," I told him sternly. But he just shrugged.

"Oh don't worry about me. As a matter of fact, I'm headed out again. But I wanted to come back and check on you, to make sure you were okay."

"What do you mean? Where are you going? What do you have to do?" I was standing by the sink. I'd been doing the dishes and my hands were wet, and as I placed them on my hips, I felt their dampness go through Scott's shirt.

"I can't tell you. The less you know, the better. That way Spaulding, Rogers, and Brewer can't get any information out of you."

"What are you talking about!"

"I have a very important appointment. That's all I can say. I'll be back later."

"Wait," I said urgently because he was turning to leave. "Scott told me to keep you here. He said it would be dangerous for you to leave."

"Can't be helped," Dr. Holdsworth interrupted briskly. "Can't miss this appointment. Too important."

He studied me for a moment, as if waiting for me to voice any final objections. But I saw it was useless and kept quiet. He turned once more to go.

"Wait," I said again. "This appointment...is it with the sorcerers?"

"The less you know, the better," he repeated, but he was grinning merrily. And in a flash, he disappeared out the door.

"I'll be damned," I said.

I finished doing the dishes. Then I brushed my teeth, got dressed, and pulled Scott's article out of my purse. By now I knew every word of it by heart. I couldn't believe I'd ever considered his philosophy childish. His contention made so much sense to me now - the world *did* need to be changed, and if not by us, then who? I put the article back into my purse. I still didn't know what I was going to do. The easiest thing to do was not think about it just yet. I still had some time.

I slipped out the door and headed for my apartment. At that point I hadn't yet decided how I'd get inside without being jumped by the thugs. So I walked very slowly, all the while trying to come up with an idea. My mind was a complete blank. Meanwhile I was getting closer and closer and closer to my place. I kept looking for Benjamin, hoping he'd turn up and protect me. But he was nowhere to be seen. I slowed my pace some more. What if the thugs came after me? What then? No one would know where to look for my bludgeoned body probably until after I'd begun to decompose. What would Scott tell my parents? "I warned her not to go," he'd say. By the time I rounded the corner, I was walking so slowly I was practically standing still.

There was a bag lady in front of my apartment, digging through the garbage that lined the curb. I hadn't put my garbage out, so I wasn't bothered by her. I'll admit that sometimes it's kind of disconcerting to throw away some old food, then look out a couple of minutes later and see someone negotiating having it for breakfast.

Anyway, I paused to watch the bag lady. There was something kind of familiar about her. Inexplicably, I felt myself head toward her. And then I recognized her.

"Myrna!"

She stood and whirled around. Her face lit up when she saw me, and I was astonished by my own pleasure at seeing her.

"Wendy! How've you been?"

"Fine, thanks. You?"

"Just fine."

For a minute we stood staring in delight at one another. I suddenly recalled that she'd done her darndest to try and get me published in a former incarnation, and decided it was time I showed my appreciation.

"Listen, Myrna, are you hungry or anything? Let me get you something to eat."

"Thanks, I'd like that very much," she said promptly, dropping a moldy roll back into the garbage.

Thank God, I thought, Now I won't have to go inside myself. It was ludicrous that I should feel safer with this tiny, feeble old bag lady with me, but for some reason, I did. I unlocked my door, and cautiously stepped inside.

To my shock, I saw that the place was in shambles. Stuff was everywhere. There were books thrown all over, drawers and cabinets were open, and the contents had all been taken out and gone through.

"I'm a terrible housekeeper," I told Myrna hastily. I didn't want her to know that some thugs were after me. But she just looked at me with a very kind smile and said I didn't have to pretend with her.

"Pretend?" I echoed. Meanwhile I was kind of poking through stuff with one toe. It didn't look as if anything was broken. Just snooped through.

"I know all about it," she said.

"All about what?"

"The sorcerers. I know all about the sorcerers."

I turned to study her, and my eyes fell upon her amulet, the one she said kept her from harm. "What exactly do you know about them," I asked carefully.

"I know that they're from another time. And that we have to help them find their way back. And that it's up to you and your friends. You're working through some karma."

Another time? Karma? I wasn't completely sure what it all meant. So I didn't say anything.

"You offered me something to eat," she reminded me.

"Oh yeah, okay." I opened the refrigerator. The thugs had finished off my beer, goddammit. There was just an egg, that jar of olives, half a loaf of bread, and nothing else. "How about a nice olive sandwich?" I asked her.

"No thanks," Myrna sighed as if to say, "I was afraid of that." I felt bad. She was looking around my kitchen, her eyes shifting through the dishes and pots and pans that covered the floor. Those bloody thugs had gone through everything. I squatted down to start to pick up the mess, but suddenly I felt overwhelmed and weak. I even felt like I might cry, something I never ever do.

"Myrna!" I wailed, "Just look at this place! Those guys have gone through everything I own! They know everything about me! They've probably read my journal and my manuscript and everything!"

I was sitting on the floor trying to hold back my tears and clean up at the same time. With a sympathetic, motherly "Oh dear!" Myrna knelt next to me and pulled my head against her bony chest. The smell of her skin was very strong, but for some reason, it didn't offend me. I allowed her to comfort me briefly, and then I became impatient and pulled away.

"Guess I should start picking this stuff up," I said.

"I'll help you," she said. I nodded doubtfully. She didn't look like she was very strong. But she worked hard and fast, and between the two of us, we got everything picked up and put away. She even washed my kitchen floor.

"Myrna, I just don't know how to thank you," I said once we'd finished. "You're so nice to me, and you don't even know me."

"Yes I do, don't you remember?"

"Oh yeah, the past life thing."

"You were very good to me once," she said, and her voice took on a new quality, kind of solemn and mysterious. She was facing me, but she seemed to be looking past me. "In our last life," she went on, "I was a young girl in trouble. I thought my boyfriend loved me, but when he got me pregnant, he disappeared. I was in disgrace. My parents insisted I move out. I was ostracized by the whole town. But you took me in. You said it didn't matter what anyone thought, that I only had to answer for myself and the child I was carrying. And even though you didn't have much money, you took care of me. You paid the midwife, and I had a healthy baby that I named after you. And in this life I gave birth to him again, and again I named him after you."

"You named your son Wendy?" I asked, baffled.

"No. Benjamin."

I was startled.

"Benjamin is your son?"

She nodded proudly. I let out a breath I didn't realize I'd been holding. It felt so weird to be talking about reincarnation with a bag lady who'd just turned down a perfectly decent olive sandwich.

"You really believe this?" I finally asked. I wasn't completely convinced myself, but I'll admit that I was on my way. She nodded and continued.

"Like I say, you took me in when everyone else shunned me. And your wife helped me raise my little-"

"Wait a minute...my wife? Do you mean to tell me that I was married to a woman in my last life?"

"Of course you were. Don't forget, you were a man then. I just told you that. Your name was Benjamin."

"Oh yeah."

"She was a lovely woman, your wife. She was very sweet tempered. To tell you the truth, I never could figure out what she saw in you."

"Thanks a bunch," I said.

"I mean, you were always kind to me, but you were very cold and unemotional. That's why you always told me not to care about what people thought of me - because you didn't care what anyone thought of you."

"I'm still that way," I said. "Tell me more about my,

um, wife."

"She was very warm and generous and affectionate. She loved everyone. And everyone loved her. Until I moved in. Then they all turned on her, and criticized her. We'd go to town, and everyone would stare at us and say terrible things about us loud enough for us to hear. I'd be in tears by the time we got home, but your wife was always cheerful and understanding and forgiving. She used to say their narrow-mindedness was their problem, not mine, and that there was no point in getting upset. Your wife helped me get over my broken heart, too, and gave me back my self esteem."

"Do you think I'll meet her in this lifetime?" I asked awkwardly. I couldn't help it. I believed every word.

"You already have. See, your souls were created at the same time, and even though you're very different, you have similar vibrations."

"Who is she?"

"Don't you know?" Myrna smiled. "She's Scott."

My eyes and mouth flew open.

"Scott? Scott was my wife?"

"Yes. Only her name was Laura then."

"Scott's name was Laura?"

"Yes. Lovely woman. Warm brown eyes and a beautiful smile that she wore all the time. When she died, you-"

"She died before me?"

"Yes."

"What happened?"

"It was so sad!" Myrna sighed. She still seemed to be looking at something past me, like she was describing a movie to me that I couldn't see. I turned around, but of course there was nothing there but my kitchen wall which had a poster of a very grim looking Nietzsche. So I turned back to Myrna, and she continued. "Laura and I went to town one afternoon. As usual, people avoided speaking to us. But Laura, she was always so friendly, she greeted everyone. Some people said hello, but most didn't say anything. Laura insisted on making a game out of it. We'd make bets on who would respond and who wouldn't, and she'd greet them to find out which of us was right. That was the only way I survived those trips into town, because I hated everyone. And it was even worse when we took Benjamin in with us. I felt sorry for him because I knew he'd suffer, too. I knew that when he was old enough to go to school he'd be teased by the other children. In fact, Laura and I were always after you to move us to another town. But you always said you didn't want to uproot yourself. You didn't care if people criticized you. Actually, I think you rather liked it. It reinforced your bitterness, and only in bitterness could you write. Your books were horribly pessimistic and morbid. Reading them was very depressing."

It was really eerie, listening to her describe me in another life. I was dismayed to realize that I hadn't changed much. I thought about Scott as Laura, cheerful, warm, and friendly.

"So how did he, I mean, how did she die?" I asked.

"I'm getting to that."

"Okay."

"Well we were in town one day. I had Benjamin with me. He'd just begun to walk. I was the typical proud mother, eager to show him off. But of course no one would even look at him. It just so happened that Sadie Lawson, the grocer's wife, was out with her son that day, too. He was the same age as Benjamin, but he wasn't walking yet. I was feeling so proud that I momentarily forgot the circumstances, and I told Sadie that it wouldn't be long before her boy was walking, too. I guess she thought I was bragging, because she said something nasty to me. She was with her friend Mary Preston, who was so thin and had such a terrible whiny voice that no one would marry her, and they both laughed. Laura and I tried to keep walking, but they began to follow us and call us names. Some other women joined them, and they were all shouting at us. It was horrible. I picked up Benjamin and tried to cover his ears. Even Laura was upset. But she just said, 'Don't listen to them. Let's go home.' So we started to head back. But as soon as we turned around, someone threw a rock. It was intended for me, but it hit Laura in the temple. She dropped to the ground, and just like that, she was dead."

I gasped. My arms were crawling with goose bumps. Myrna had begun to sniff a little, so I reached out and patted her on the shoulder. It was very upsetting to think that Scott had been killed by a mob of angry bitches in his last lifetime. Myrna took a deep, unsteady breath, and finished her story.

"Anyway, after Laura died, we finally moved, you and I and Benjamin. Of course it wasn't proper for us to be living together if we weren't married, so you took me for your wife. But you were never the same again. You tried to work, but everything you wrote was bizarre and full of hate and despair. You finally committed suicide."

"I did?"

"Yes. You drowned yourself."

I felt such a hot rush go through me that I thought for a minute I was going to faint or throw up. For as long as I can remember, I've had a violent fear of water. I can still remember summers when I was young and the weather was hot and all the other kids would go swimming. I would stand and watch them, but I'd never go in myself. Not ever. They'd tease me, but I didn't care - getting teased was better than going in the water. I'd always come up with some excuse, like I had an ear infection or a cold or something. When I got older I'd say I was getting my period. During the summer I was getting my period about every week. Once my brother picked me up and threw me into the pool. I screamed and got sick and passed out, and wound up spending the next two days in bed. I didn't even like to get baths when I was a baby - my mother had to sponge me clean because I always screamed when she put me in the tub. So when Myrna said I'd drown myself, and I knew there was no way she could possibly know about my fear of water, I gave up trying to be skeptical.

"I must have really loved her," I said.

"You did. But you never showed it. After she died, you worried that she never knew how you felt about her, because you never took the time to tell her. You weren't the type of man who would talk about caring for someone. And that's why you killed yourself. You couldn't live with the guilt anymore. You used to say you would do *anything* if you could see her just once more and tell her how much you loved her."

Finally Myrna fell silent. Neither of us said anything for a while. I was thinking about my feelings for Scott. Myrna's story explained why I'd been so in love with him even before I met him - I guess I remembered being in love with him in my last life. I wondered if he remembered. What if he didn't love me back in this life? What if he was paying me back for those years of cold, unaffectionate companionship? I shuddered.

"Myrna, thanks for...thanks for helping me clean my apartment," I said. "Look, I have to leave now. Can I do anything for you? I mean, do you need anything? I don't have much money, but why don't you take some."

I reached into my purse. She started to shake her head, but I took out all I had, $11, and pressed it into her hand.

"You don't have to-"

"I want to," I said. "I can't imagine what it must be like to have no money for food and no place to live. I mean, where do you sleep at night?"

Myrna stared at the money I'd given her for a moment, then she sighed unhappily.

"Well, Benjamin and I have been staying at a shelter for the homeless. But it was condemned this morning. I'm not sure where we'll stay now."

"Hey, I wonder if...no, that's no good," I murmured.

"What."

"Well, I was going to suggest that you stay here. But obviously you wouldn't be safe here.

Myrna's eyes lit up at my suggestion, even after I'd reminded her of the danger.

"Wendy! Could we really stay here?"

"But the thugs-"

"Oh, they probably won't be back. They know you're not here anymore, and they've already gone through your things and not found what they were looking for. Why would they want to come back? I'm sure we'd be safe here."

She was staring at me urgently. I was doubtful. What if something happened to her?

"Don't forget, I have this," she reminded me, tapping her amulet.

"Come on, Myrna! A necklace isn't going to be any kind of protection when those three guys show up. They could kill you."

"Not while I have this," she insisted. "Please, Wendy? I promise I'll keep your place neat, and it'll only be for a few days, until Benjamin and I find somewhere to live.

I hesitated for a second longer. But she was regarding me with such hopeful eyes that I couldn't turn her down.

"Okay," I said reluctantly, "but *please* be careful. Keep the door locked. Don't let anyone in."

"Don't worry," she said, and then she laughed gaily, like a young girl. I couldn't resist patting her arm, and then I actually kind of hugged her. From a mug in one of my cabinets I took out a spare key and gave it to her.

"Here. Be careful," I told her again. She promised that she would as she walked me to the door.

"Thank you so much, Wendy. I know Benjamin will be grateful, too."

"You're welcome. I just hope you'll be okay here."

"I will! Don't worry about me."

"Okay."

Our eyes met, and we both smiled.

"Goodbye," I said.

"Goodbye. You be careful, too, honey."

I told her I would, and walked out. I looked up and down the street for the thugs, but didn't see them anywhere. So I walked for a little while, pondering what Myrna had told me about being married to Scott in a previous life. And suddenly I was determined to do whatever I had to in order to get him to marry me again, in this life. Suddenly that was even more important than finding the sorcerers.

CHAPTER THREE

I decided to do some shopping, so I went up to a money machine, inserted my card, and withdrew $50. After I'd tucked it into my wallet, I compared the balance according to the computer to the number I'd written in my book, and as usual, they weren't at all alike. But for once the discrepancy was in my favor. From there I went to a CVS to look at the make-up. There were more kinds than I ever would have dreamed possible - there were a zillion different shades of blush and lipstick and eye shadow - and all at an everyday low price. I didn't know where to begin. So I prowled up and down the aisle for several minutes, looking at everything but not touching anything. I watched what other women bought and studied their faces, and finally bought myself a subtle blush, some black mascara, and a case with twelve different colored pads of eye shadow that looked just like a water color set I used to have when I was about seven years old. Then I went to a grocery store and got stuff to make a nice dinner for Scott when he got home. And Dr. Holdsworth, too, of course.

I took everything back to Scott's place, put the food away, and jumped into the shower for the better part of an hour. Then, wrapping up my hair in a towel, I looked at my face in the mirror. I cursed my features for being so unremarkable. But at least my complexion was good. I tried the blush first, put way too much on, and wound up having to wipe it off twice before I got it right. Brushing on the mascara was a bitch. I'd only done it a couple of times in my entire life, and my hand shook so much I was afraid I'd poke my eye out. Then I put the slightest hint of blue shadow, not on my lid, but above it, just below my eye brow. Turning my face this way and that, I admired the outcome. I'm not going to say that I was instantly transformed into a raving beauty, but I looked a tiny bit better. All in all, I was pleased. I dried my hair as much as I could with the towel, then scrunched and fluffed it with my fingers. It fell, dark and curly, to the middle of my back. I wondered if Scott liked long hair or if he preferred those snappy little haircuts that real fashionable women sport. I decided that if he asked me to cut it, I would.

All the while I kept glancing at the clock and pondering what Dr. Holdsworth had told me that morning. I was concerned that I hadn't heard from him again. What was Scott going to say when he found out I let Dr. Holdsworth out of my sight? As I passed Scott's tape deck, I pressed "power" and then "play," and waited to hear what would come out. It was some of that new music that was reminiscent of the folk music of the sixties. Normally I wouldn't have liked it, but at that moment it sounded really good, so I left it on, and started to straighten up the apartment a bit.

A little while later the phone rang. I didn't know if I should answer it or not. What if it was some girl looking for Scott? I decided to let it ring. On the other hand, what if it was Scott? I picked up the receiver and said, "Hello," in a sexy, husky voice I use occasionally. There was a silence at the other end, then I heard Scott say, "Wendy?"

"Yes," I said.

"Are you okay? You sound funny."

"I'm fine," I said.

"Good. I'm calling to find out how everything is going. What are you and Dr. Holdsworth up to?"

"Dr. Holdsworth isn't here."

"What? What do you mean? Where is he?"

"I don't know. He snuck out early this morning while I was asleep. I don't know where he went." I waited apprehensively. Scott had given me a single assignment, and I'd fucked up. When he didn't say anything, I added, "Scott, I'm pretty sure he's safe."

"Why?"

"Because I think he's with the sorcerers."

"What? Really?"

"I think so. He told me he had a very important appointment."

"When?"

"This afternoon."

"No, I mean, when did he tell you that? I thought you said he left while you were asleep."

"He did. But then he came back to check on me. Only for a second, Scott - I tried to stop him from going out again, honest! But he insisted. He said he had an appointment that was too important for him to miss. I think he was going to meet the sorcerers."

"Son of a bitch," Scott's voice was low and impressed. "Look, I have to go now. I'll be home around 7:00 or so. Okay?"

"Okay. You'll be home for dinner, right?" I couldn't help smiling as I said that. It sounded like he was smiling, too, and he told me he would be.

"Good. See you then," I said, and hung up. Suddenly I felt wonderful. I couldn't remember when I'd felt so deeply in love. Probably never. I'd had lots of boyfriends, but I'd never considered marrying any of them, even the ones I'd gone out with for a long time, like a year or something. I'd even lived with guys I had no intention of marrying. But Scott was different from anyone else I'd every known. He was so relentlessly optimistic. He reminded me of the way I used to be before I graduated from college and learned how shitty the world is. But Scott acted as if he'd never learned that. I couldn't help it, I found myself wanting to be like him.

I made a four layer lasagna and put it in the oven. Then all at once I realized I hadn't had a cigarette in a long time. Reaching into my purse for a pack, I pulled out instead my rebuttal to Scott's article.

"Shit, forgot all about this," I muttered, swiftly reading through the words I'd written. Suddenly they seemed childishly pessimistic, like a kid in a store who wants his mother to buy candy for him, and then cries when she doesn't. Scott's article, on the other hand, struck me as being somehow more mature. I tore up what I'd written, buried it in the garbage, and wondered if I should quit writing for *The No Frills Dirt*.

A knock on the door startled me.

"Who is it," I demanded, rising and looking desperately around for the knife I'd used to cut up the onions for the sauce.

"Don't panic, it's only me," I heard Scott's voice say gently. I looked at the clock. It wasn't even 6:00. He was early! Delighted, I unlocked the door and let him in.

"How was your day, dear?" I joked.

"Fine, dear. How was your day?"

I debated whether or not to tell him that I'd spent part of the day learning that we'd been married in our last life, and that he'd been killed by a mob of angry women, and that I'd committed suicide because I couldn't live without him.

"Fine," I said. "Dinner will be ready in a few minutes. You want a beer?"

Scott nodded gratefully. Meanwhile, he was unbuttoning his shirt and peeling it off as he headed for his room.

"Any word from Dr. Holdsworth?" I heard him call.

"Um, no," I felt guilty about that, even though I knew Scott didn't blame me. He reappeared a second later, wearing green gym shorts and a t-shirt with cows on it.

"Wow, something smells great!" he said, opening up the oven door and peeking inside. "Lasagna! Did you make that?" I could tell he was surprised. Probably thought I couldn't cook. Actually, I don't very often. But I can always pull off a respectable lasagna.

"The sorcerers must have made it. I went out for a while, and when I came back, it was already in the oven, cooking away."

Scott shut the oven door and stared at me.

"Really?"

I smiled. He realized I was kidding, and smiled too, and said that nothing would surprise him anymore. I fetched him a beer from the refrigerator and he popped it open. We both sat at the kitchen table, and I automatically reached out for a sip. Even though I'd bought plenty of beer, it seemed more comfortable to be sharing a can.

"So, what did you do today?" he asked.

"Well, I ran into Myrna."

"The bag lady?"

"Yeah," I nodded. "Guess what I found out? She's

Benjamin's mother."

"She is?"

"Yeah."

"Huh. What else did she say?"

"She said that she knows all about the sorcerers. And she helped me clean my apartment. The thugs made a real mess of it. Hey, Scott?"

"Hmm?"

"Do you believe in reincarnation"

Scott was surprised by my question. He'd only been half listening to me talk about Myrna; he'd been checking his watch every couple of minutes and glancing at the door, obviously hoping Dr. Holdsworth would show up. When I mentioned reincarnation, though, I really snagged his attention.

"Why do you ask?" he said.

"Well, Myrna and I talked about it today. I've never believed in it before. In fact, I've always been kind of scornful of anyone who did. But now I'm not so sure."

"Why? What did she say."

"Just different stuff," I answered vaguely. Somehow I didn't feel right telling him we'd been married. I was afraid he'd think I was just saying that so that he'd feel obligated to fall in love with me again, and besides, I didn't want him to know I was in love with him. I mean, I kind of wanted him to know, but I didn't *really* want him to know. So I just shrugged and said I'd been a writer in my last life, too.

"Really? Who."

"Someone who never got published."

"Oh."

"So do you, Scott?"

He wasn't at all embarrassed as he nodded.

"Yeah, I do. It makes so much sense to me. I mean, I

can't even remember a time when I didn't believe I'd come back after I died. When I was real young, I assumed it was something everyone believed, I assumed it was an established fact. I mean, this was even before I knew there was a name for it. Once, I guess I was in the second grade or something, I carved my initials into my desk, so that when I came back in my next life I'd be able to recognize my desk and sit there again. The teacher caught me and I got into big trouble. She said I was defacing school equipment. I tried to explain, but she wouldn't listen. She told me to stop being so silly, that when we die, we go to heaven or hell, depending on the way we behave on earth. She even said I'd go to hell if I wasn't more careful. That was when I realized not everyone thought as I did. That was my first experience with close mindedness. I mean, she was absolutely convinced that she was right. She wouldn't even for a second consider that what I thought might have some validity. She ridiculed me in front of the whole class. I cried all the way home. But when I told my mother, she said that was just the way some people were, and that it didn't make sense to worry about them. And she was right, you know. There are always going to be people who disagree with you, no matter what you believe."

"Uh huh," I said. He seemed so wise. I felt stupid and young.

"So when will dinner be done?" he asked abruptly. "I'm starving."

I got up and took the lasagna out of the oven. It weighed about a ton. I dished out a huge piece for Scott, and a more modest serving for myself. Then I took out a salad I'd made, and sliced the French bread I'd bought at a bakery. It was a very nice meal.

"You look different to me," Scott said midway through

dinner. At first I didn't have any idea what he was talking about. Then I remembered the make-up. I felt unbearably sheepish. I mean, I wanted him to notice that I was wearing it, but I guess I wanted him to fall in love with me without commenting on my new face. So I just shrugged and tried to change the subject.

"Wonder if we should call Delores tonight."

"You look really nice," he said. My skin felt as if it was on fire. I looked away so that he wouldn't see me blushing. He could tell I was embarrassed, so he said casually, "Yeah, I'll give her a call after dinner." Then, while he had seconds on everything, we fell to discussing Dr. Holdsworth and the sorcerers. I was telling Scott that I'd had another nightmare, when all at once the door flew open and Dr. Holdsworth burst in. Scott and I leapt from our seats and demanded to know where he'd been.

"I can't talk right now," he told us breathlessly. "I just wanted to stop in and tell you that it's more important than ever that we don't divulge the whereabouts of the sorcerers. I'm amazed at the knowledge they possess! Knowledge that, if in the wrong hands, could destroy the world!"

"What do you mean? What knowledge?" Scott and I asked together. But Dr. Holdsworth shook his head, sat down, helped himself to a slab of lasagna, and said he had to be leaving again soon.

"But Dr. Holdsworth, shouldn't you keep out of sight? Those thugs are bound to see you," I said, concerned.

"No need to worry," he said. "Mmm, good lasagna."

"What do you mean?"

"Well the noodles are perfect, and the sauce has just the right amount of-"

"No, I mean, why shouldn't we worry?"

"Oh." Dr. Holdsworth grinned, and from his pocket he withdrew a small, smooth, white stone that had a black spot inside, right in the center, like the dark pupil of an eye. "Because I've got this."

"What's that?"

"It's belocolus. It prevents me from being seen. The sorcerers gave it to me."

Scott and I exchanged doubtful, silent glances.

"I'm telling you, it makes me invisible to them," Dr. Holdsworth insisted. He was going to offer to show us the stone, but instead he dropped it back into his pocket.

"But how can-"

"Okay, don't believe me! I don't care! If you knew the sorcerers, you'd understand!"

"Dr. Holdsworth," Scott said suddenly in a voice so firm it surprised me, "I think it's time you leveled with us. If you want us to help you, you have to tell us what we're up against. First you said there were no sorcerers. Now you're telling us that they've given you a rock that makes you invisible. I think it's only fair you take a minute and tell us what the hell is going on!"

I nodded in full agreement. Dr. Holdsworth looked appropriately chastised, realized that Scott was absolutely right, and nodded.

"Let's hear it," I urged.

"On one condition," he said, and lifted his eyes to meet ours.

"What."

"That you keep an open mind about the things I'm about to say. Don't laugh or anything. Listen to the whole story, and reserve judgement until the end. Okay?"

"Okay," we said together, "Go ahead."

CHAPTER FOUR

Dr. Holdsworth heaved a preparatory sigh and leaned back in his chair, but then immediately leaned forward again, to rest his hands on the table. He regarded us very seriously.

"This is how it began," he said. "I'd just released my book, *Creating The Magic Within Yourself,* which, as you know, deals quite extensively with some ancient sorcerers who, I claimed, had power because they *believed* they had power. Well the book hadn't been out a month when I received a very strange phone call from someone asking me all kinds of questions about my research. He told me I'd made a couple of mistakes, and wanted to know if I'd be interested in getting together to discuss them. 'You might say I'm an expert on sorcerers,' he said. To tell you the truth, it rubbed me the wrong way. I'm a scrupulous researcher, and I'd very carefully consulted with hundreds of reliable sources. I told the man this, and cited some of the books I'd used. 'I've read them, too,' he said, 'and they're full of errors.' He was so sure of himself that I became curious. We arranged a meeting time. He seemed reluctant to appear anywhere in public, and offered to come by my house late the following evening. I was a little suspicious, but I agreed. Then, just before we hung up, he said very enthusiastically, 'Wonderful invention, the telephone.' I couldn't imagine why he'd say something like that. All I could think was that it was the kind of thing you'd say if you'd never used a phone before.

"I'd given him very explicit directions to my house, but I wasn't sure he'd be able to find me. He seemed totally unfamiliar with any landmarks, and was vague as to where he was coming from. Just before 10:00 I turned on the light, and stood by the door watching for him out the window. I was sure he'd get lost. But just as my grandfather clock began to strike the hour, there was a loud knocking on the door. Low on the door. It startled me, because like I say, I was standing right there looking out and hadn't seen anyone arrive. And I still didn't see anyone. So I opened the door, and standing there on my porch were three tiny men. They had long white beards, and they were wearing robes and pointed caps. Well obviously my first thought was that someone was playing a joke on me. It was no secret that I'd been researching sorcerers - what would be funnier than having three of them appear on my porch? So I burst out laughing. I said something like, 'Oh, very good! You've got the costumes just right!' or something, and I expected them to laugh with me. But they didn't. They just stood there, looking up at me with blue eyes as bright as lights on a Christmas tree. Anyway, I invited them in, and they scurried past me. I still thought it was a very clever joke, so I watched them carefully. I was particularly struck by their eyes, which as I said before, were quite an amazing blue. I thought they must be wearing some kind of iridescent lenses, but I couldn't tell for sure. They impressed me as being very childlike in their delight with everything in the room. I have lots of rare artifacts I've picked up from all parts of the world, and those three little men were fascinated, and spoke excitedly amongst themselves for several minutes in voices too low for me to hear. Their enthusiasm was somehow refreshing. You see, no matter how old something I've got is, or how rare, I'm used to colleagues telling me they've got one that's older or more rare. So it was a pleasure to watch the three of them dashing around my living room. Eventually they assembled themselves into a half circle before me, and commenced to stare up at me with those blazing blue eyes.

"'I am Cozlu,' said one. The tallest one introduced himself as Puu. Then to my surprise that last one, who wore a big grin, gave me a Peace sign and said his name was Bni. 'That's B-n-i,' he said, 'The B is, as you say, silent.'"

"He gave you a Peace sign? Like this?" Scott asked, holding up the two appropriate fingers. Dr. Holdsworth nodded.

"Yes. Bni has a deep interest in the paradigm shift that took place in the sixties. His vocabulary is sprinkled with phrases characteristic of that era. It's pretty strange, listening to him speak, but you get used to it. Anyway, I told them to make themselves at home, and offered them tea. Puu and Bni looked at Cozlu - he seemed to be the eldest and the one in charge - and he nodded and said they'd like that very much. I suggested they have a seat, and like children they climbed onto my couch. Their feet didn't touch the floor, and they folded their hands solemnly in their laps, patiently awaiting their tea. I laughed again. I mean, I still thought it was a joke, and I was trying to think who'd set it up. They were really convincing because they weren't holding back giggles or anything. They were perfectly serious. I told them I'd be right back, and went into the kitchen. While I heated up the water for the tea, I sneaked back to the doorway of the living room and peeked at them; I figured they be laughing. But they weren't. They were dashing all over, whispering excitedly and holding up the different artifacts. They reminded me of people from a depressed country seeing America for the first time. They were quite taken with my calculator, and I heard Puu say that it must be one of those 'space age computers.' I watched them until the tea kettle began to whistle. It startled them so much that they threw themselves back on the couch. When I came into the room with three cups of tea, they were sitting exactly as I'd left them, with their hands folded in their laps. I served them, and all three promptly burned their tongues. It looked as if they'd had no experience with drinking hot liquids before, and they set the cups back on the saucers and didn't drink anymore.

"'Too much caffeine can be a real drag,' Bni said. I said that was certainly true, then suggested we get down to business. I asked them what they could tell me about sorcerers.

"'We can tell you everything about sorcerers," Cozlu said in a very high pitched, regal voice, "because we *are* sorcerers.' 'No!' I said, feigning surprise, 'Really?' 'Really!' all three said at once. They told me they'd read my book, and had been impressed by it. They were pleased that I'd emphasized the importance of believing in one's powers.

"'That's the problem with your modern society,' Cozlu said, 'You have never learned to believe in your own abilities. You let machines or other people do all kinds of things you could be doing for yourself, and this renders you essentially powerless. You're all caught in a trap of your own design, and you don't even realize it.' I asked him to explain further, and he said, 'You've all alienated yourselves from yourselves. You work in an office environment all day, performing tasks for some huge corporation, then you go home and surrender your mind to a television set. You don't spend time with yourselves, and that's terribly unhealthy.' And he said that after they'd read my book, they'd decided to come to me and ask for my help. 'We can tell you're a thinking man,' he said, 'and we don't have anyone else to turn to.' Bni said, 'We've been doing some heavy duty freaking.' I asked them what they meant, what kind of help did they need. And that's when they told me they were from a different time."

"Oh yeah, that's right, a different time," I interrupted. Dr. Holdsworth and Scott looked at me curiously, and I explained that Myrna had said something about that.

"Now I'm a scientist," Dr. Holdsworth went on. "and while I've always considered time travel to be a viable possibility, I never expected to see evidence of it on my living room couch. So I waited while they told me how it happened. Seems that Bni read the wrong spell during a ritual, and they wound up here, in present day Boston. So they'd come to me, hoping I could help them go back in time. Mind you, I still didn't believe they were actually sorcerers. But the more I watched them and listened to them, the more I kind of got caught up in the idea that maybe they were. There was something so convincing about their manner. I found myself wanting to believe them. So I put aside my doubts for the time being, and decided to act as if they really were sorcerers.

"'We need to find our handbook,' Cozlu said, 'in order to reverse the spell.' I asked where that was, and they explained that during the travel through time, the book had somehow disappeared. 'Because of its chemical structure and its magical power,' Puu speculated, 'it probably travelled at a different rate, and arrived sooner than us.' I asked them how much sooner, but they said they didn't have any idea. 'Time travel isn't really our bag, man,' Bni told me. So I asked them how they thought I could help, and Cozlu said that since I had Ph.D.'s in Astronomy, Archeology, and Physics, maybe I could calculate the location of the handbook, taking into consideration the time difference, the position of the earth, and so on.' 'What if someone has already found the book,' I asked them, 'What then?' But they said it was just a chance they had to take. And they looked so unhappy that I said I'd try. I think by this time I'd pretty much accepted them as authentic sorcerers.

"We sat up for the rest of the night, going over the conditions for the past 3000 years. Of course they couldn't say exactly when they'd lived - their calendar is entirely different from ours. But we had a few bits of information to work with. They told me about tools and climate and that kind of thing, and we were able to narrow it down. It still represented a lot of calculations, of course. But just before dawn all three of them leapt up from the couch simultaneously, said they had to be going, and disappeared out the door. And I mean, they disappeared. They stood at the door, muttered something, and just like that, they were gone. Well that really blew my mind, as Bni would say. I went to bed for a few hours, and when I woke up, I was sure it had all been a dream. But then I went into my living room and saw those three cups of tea, and I knew it had really happened.

"I worked the whole next day on the problem. There were hundreds of possibilities that had to be taken into consideration. The next time I looked up, it was dark out. I'd reached a snag in my calculations, and needed to take a break. I suddenly realized I hadn't eaten all day, nor gotten much sleep the night before. But instead of going to a restaurant, I wound up at a bar. I figured it would clear my head."

"You figured that going to a bar would clear your head?" I asked curiously. Dr. Holdsworth smiled and nodded.

"That's what alcohol does for me. It tends to inhibit the rational left half of my brain and liberates my more imaginative right half. I thought if I could get just a little bit drunk, I'd be able to view the problem from a different perspective, and solve it. It's a method that's always worked for me. So I left the house, walked up the street to a nearby bar, and ordered a whiskey. Sure enough, as soon as I drank it my thoughts got a little clearer. Like I said, that's how alcohol affects me. Unfortunately, it also makes me more talkative. I ordered another whiskey, and another, and before too long, I heard myself telling the bartender all about these sorcerers. He kept saying, 'Yeah, sure, buddy,' and I knew he didn't believe me, but I didn't care. I started talking about the powers the sorcerers had, and how they could change the weather and that kind of thing. Suddenly a man tapped me on the arm, and he seemed very interested in what I was saying.

"'You've actually met these sorcerers?' he asked. I told him I had, ordered another drink, and told him that I was doing some work for them. He began to ask all kinds of questions about their powers, if they could influence the stock market or predict the lottery. I said I didn't know. I should have dismissed him then and there, and gone back to work. But I didn't. I agreed to go back to his office with him. He paid for my drinks, and hailed a taxi. I passed out on the way over, and the next thing I knew, I was being dragged up some stairs. We'd been joined by two other men. I was feeling sick and dizzy and asked them to take me home. But they said not until I told them everything. 'Drink this,' said one of them, 'It will make you feel better.' I guess it was more whiskey. Anyway, I drank it. Then they asked me some more questions. They kept filling my glass, and I kept talking. I can't really remember what I told them. It seems like I talked all night. I vaguely remember them loading me into a taxi and taking me home. I woke up the next day with the worst hangover of my life."

"Those three guys - Spaulding, Rogers, and Brewer, right?" I said.

"Right. Anyway, they showed up at my house a couple of days later and asked if I remembered talking to them. I said I did. I apologized for getting drunk. I told them I'd been lying, and that there really weren't any sorcerers. But they said they'd seen papers on my desk full of calculations about time travel. So they said they knew I was up to something. I told them to leave me alone, but they insisted on knowing where the sorcerers were. I told them I didn't know, which I didn't, but they didn't believe me. They tried to force me to tell them. Gave me a black eye. Almost broke my arm. But when I kept saying that I didn't know, they finally let up on me. 'We'll be back,' they said. And as Wendy can attest, they were."

"They're trouble," I said.

"But Dr. Holdsworth," Scott said, "What about the sorcerers?"

"Well," said Dr. Holdsworth, "I've met with them several times since then, and we've determined the location of the book."

"You have? Where is it?" Scott demanded breathlessly. I could see he was completely convinced. He hadn't seen the sorcerers or the thugs, but he believed every word. He amazed me.

"The book is located under Wendy's kitchen floor," Dr. Holdsworth announced.

Scott and I stared in surprise at Dr. Holdsworth, then at each other, and then back at Dr. Holdsworth again.

"You're kidding," I said.

"No. According to my calculations, it's buried right in the center of your kitchen floor. When I told the sorcerers, Cozlu said, 'That means she's in danger, too,' and he and Puu and Bni decided to do something about it."

"They sent Myrna and Benjamin to warn me," I said.

"Exactly. They wanted you to know ahead of time to be careful. But of course it wasn't yet clear as to what kind of danger you would be in, or how much you would be involved."

"But how did the sorcerers know Myrna and Benjamin?"

"Apparently Myrna and Benjamin were the first people the sorcerers encountered. Of course the sorcerers couldn't speak English, and Myrna and Benjamin couldn't speak *Knidusi*, which is the language of the sorcerers, but through gestures, Myrna made it clear that she wanted to invite them back to her room at the shelter and gave them something to eat. Even though she didn't have much food, she was willing to share what was there. Originally, the sorcerers assumed that that kind of generosity was typical of people here. But they soon learned differently. One afternoon some kids threw some rocks at them. And they've been chased by dogs on several occasions. Anyway, Myrna and Benjamin told the sorcerers where they were and what year it was. Myrna told them that she possessed very little knowledge herself, and suggested that they go to a library to learn about all that had happened since their time. The sorcerers were so grateful to her that they made her an amulet, which they told her would keep her from harm."

"I saw it," I said. "Benjamin has one, too."

"Yes. Benjamin was very helpful as well - he took them to my house that first night. Anyway, this was when I started staying in the house with the doors locked and the shades down. I met with the sorcerers every night - they could sneak in without being seen, they said, because they had powers that protected them from harm. We were trying to figure out a plan that would get us into your place, Wendy. Obviously I couldn't show up at your door with a shovel and ask if I could dig up your kitchen floor. Imagine my shock when you showed up at my door! And when you invited me to stay at your place, I thought, This is too good to be true! That was why I tried to get you all to leave right away - I wanted to start digging. But unfortunately our friends showed up before I had the chance."

"I can't believe the book is buried beneath my kitchen floor," I shook my head in amazement.

"If no one has moved it," Dr. Holdsworth clarified.

"Let's go over there right now and look for it," Scott said, and he was already up on his feet.

"Wait," I said, "What about the thugs? Surely they're watching the place."

"They can't see me, because I have this," Dr. Holdsworth once again pulled out his stone. "Tell you what - I'll see if I can get some for you two."

Even Scott looked doubtful. As for me, I almost said, "Let's just forget the whole thing." I mean, what good could carrying a stone possibly do?

"You have to believe," Dr. Holdsworth said.

"I don't know," I said frankly.

"Then I'll just go by myself," he said, and rose as if he intended to do just that. "That's where I was going anyway, until you stopped me."

"Just wait," I said, yanking him back into his seat, and Scott too. I wanted to think about it all. I mean, if I really believed that a stone had the power to protect me...*could* it? How could something like belief actually impair someone's vision? How could such a thing be possible?

I was about to shake my head, when Scott said suddenly, "Count me in, Dr. Holdsworth. I believe you."

"You do?" My eyes opened wide. Was he crazy? Then I remembered how open minded he was, and I remembered that I was trying to be like him. But I couldn't force myself to believe something that deep down I knew was ludicrous. Could I? I wished I could. But I just couldn't. I couldn't believe that carrying some stone would prevent me from being seen. It was too illogical.

"I'll get you a stone, Scott," I heard Dr. Holdsworth say. I looked up and saw that once again they were both hovering by the door.

"Listen up," I said, "if anyone is going to dig up my kitchen floor, I'm going to be there, stone or no stone. Maybe I can hide behind one of you," I added, which of course made absolutely no sense at all. It was as if I believed that they could carry a stone and not be seen, but I couldn't believe it about myself. No matter how hard I tried, I just couldn't.

"Let's do it," Scott urged. "Dr. Holdsworth, go get us some stones."

Dr. Holdsworth nodded briskly and was out the door in a second. Off to get us stones that would prevent us from being seen.

"I just hope this works," I said grimly.

CHAPTER FIVE

The phone rang suddenly, startling us. We looked at it, and it rang again. Scott reached over and said, "Hello?" into the receiver. I didn't even bother to not listen in. "Hey," he said, "how are you?" He mouthed the word "Delores" to me, and I nodded. She apparently said she was fine, because Scott said he was fine, too, and pretty soon he was telling her about all that had happened.

"Well, okay," I heard him say, "But make sure you're not being followed, okay? Okay. See you." He hung up and said that she was on her way over.

"I wonder if she'll need a stone too," I said, but Scott didn't answer. He seemed to be lost in thought. I pretended to be lost in thought, too, but actually I was studying him. He was staring past me, tapping one finger on the table. I noticed that his nails were very short and very neat, with very even white moons. He wore no jewelry. Dark brown hair, beginning at the wrist, made its way up his arm and disappeared beneath his shirt. I love a man with hairy arms. My skin tingled a little, and I had to look away.

"Hey Wendy," he said abruptly.

"What."

"What do you think of all of this? Do you think Dr.

Holdsworth is out of his mind, or what? Do you believe everything he says?"

"I'm not sure. It would be easy for me to, because I've seen the sorcerers myself. On the other hand, it's pretty bizarre. I think I want to wait around and see what develops. I'm not sure about this whole stone thing, though."

"I am," he admitted, "and it scares me. I mean, how can an intelligent, well read, 20th century guy like me believe that carrying a stone can mean the difference between being seen and not being seen? It's ridiculous. But I can't help it. I do believe it. I guess I want to."

"I'll tell you, Scott," I said, "I wish I felt that way. I wish I could open up my mind the way you do. But I can't. And if I don't believe in the powers of this silly stone, they'll see me. And if they see me, they'll see you guys, too. And then we'll all be in trouble. I just don't know what to say, Scott. But I'm willing to give it a try."

"Good. As soon as Dr. Holdsworth gets back with the stones, we'll head over to your place."

"Okay."

"Okay."

The question, "In the meantime, what should we do?" hung heavy in the air, thick and fragrant as the lasagna sitting still warm on the oven. Scott's hand stopped tapping all at once, and crept across the table and covered mine.

"Imagine if you have never come here that night," he said, smiling. "I'd probably be sitting here all alone with nothing to do. In fact, I'd probably have stayed at work. I usually work about sixty hours a week, because I just don't have much else to do. I guess I'm kind of lonely."

I was surprised. He was so friendly. How was it possible that he was lonely? But before I could comment, there was a sudden knock on the door. Once again, Scott and I were startled. We were both very jumpy, as if we'd just had a dozen cups of coffee each.

"She made good time," Scott said, opening the door to let Delores in. But it wasn't Delores at all. It was Benjamin.

"They know who I am," he said, "And they're after me."

"What? Tell us what happened," Scott said, closing and locking the door. "Did they follow you here?"

"No, I think I lost them. Wow, that lasagna smells good."

"Sit down," I said, and served him a big piece of it. I decided that I'd bring the rest of it back to my apartment, so that Myrna could have some, too.

"What happened?" Scott asked again.

"Well," said Benjamin in between mouthfuls, "They know that Mother and I are staying at your place. Hey, thanks a lot, by the way."

"You are?" Scott asked. I'd forgotten to tell him that I'd offered Myrna and Benjamin my apartment. I nodded. "Will they be safe there?"

I said that I didn't know, and that I'd tried to talk Myrna out of staying there.

"Mother and I will be fine," Benjamin assured us. "We got amulets. Remember?"

Scott and I exchanged doubtful glances.

"Besides," Benjamin concluded, "What else can we do, sleep in the street? How much safer would that be?"

Scott started to say that Benjamin and his mother were welcome to stay with him, but Benjamin shook his head and tapped his amulet, just the way Myrna had. So Scott shrugged and said okay.

"Anyway," Benjamin went on, "I was leaving the

apartment when all of a sudden I spotted them standing a couple of paces up the street. They saw me, too, and headed for me. I ran away as fast as I could. I'm pretty sure I lost them."

Before Scott and I could comment on that, there was another knock at the door.

"That must be Delores," said Scott. And sure enough, when he opened the door she burst in.

"Tell me everything that's been going on," she said. She sat in the only remaining empty seat. Wordlessly, I served her some lasagna, which she ate as she waited for news.

"I don't believe we've met," Benjamin said, and his voice was very gentle. Delores regarded him curiously, but shook his hand when he extended it.

"Delores, this is Benjamin."

"The mad man you were telling me about?" she asked, then clamped her hand over her mouth. "I'm sorry! That was so rude of me!"

"That's okay," Benjamin smiled, and he wasn't in the least bit offended. He was studying Delores, and I tried to see her with his eyes. She looked very pretty, with her eyes bright with excitement, and her delicate pink nails. She was wearing a white blouse and a peach skirt, and she had her hair tied back in a peach bow. Around her neck was a peach and white coral necklace, and even her earrings were peach colored. I was impressed. It would just never occur to me to coordinate my outfit like that. I wondered if Scott was admiring her, too, or just looking at her like a friend. She turned back to Scott and insisted again that he fill her in. So he did, beginning with my run in with the thugs, and concluding with the information that the sorcerers' handbook was buried under my kitchen floor.

157

"I don't believe it, that's amazing!" she said, nodding as I offered her more lasagna.

"It really happened," I assured her. "And these thugs are mean. I hope you don't have to deal with them."

"I hope not, too! Well, so now what?"

"Well, now we're waiting for Dr. Holdsworth to come back. Then we're going over to Wendy's to start digging," Scott said.

The words were no sooner out of his mouth than the door burst open, and Dr. Holdsworth came in.

"Got them!" he said excitedly. Then his eyes fell upon Delores, and he stopped dead in his tracks. She rose to greet him with her warm smile. I really admired it. It had a strong effect on Dr. Holdsworth. He smiled back, but was suddenly very shy, and ducked his head. I knew he was thinking she looked beautiful. I looked down to see what I was wearing that day, and saw that it was my "Shit happens" t-shirt. When this is over I'm going to get myself some new clothes, I thought.

"You got the stones?"

"Yes." From his pocket, Dr. Holdsworth withdrew a couple of them.

"What are those?" Delores and Benjamin asked together.

"Belocolus," Dr. Holdsworth, "They'll keep us from being seen. Only I don't have enough for everyone. Oh well, some of us will have to share."

"Will that work?" I asked.

"I don't know. We'll have to see, won't we. Everyone ready to go?"

Scott and Benjamin and Delores and I exchanged looks. We were either going to be able to sneak into my place unnoticed by killer thugs, locate an ancient handbook of magic, and send a trio of sorcerers back to their own time, or we were going to die.

"We're ready," I affirmed.

PART FOUR

PROLOGUE

"Cozlu, do you think Dr. Holdsworth will be able to help us find our way back?" Puu asked. He and Bni stared hopefully at the eldest sorcerer.

"I could sure dig that," Bni added mournfully.

"Well, now that we know the exact location of The Great Book, *we can dig it up and can use it to send ourselves back in time, provided no one has moved it."*

"What if someone has?" moaned Puu.

Cozlu frowned and said, "Well, in that case, perhaps he can think of something else. He's very bright. He seems to have attended several highly esteemed colleges."

The three little men were sitting beneath a bush along the edge of the Common. It was a chilly night - summer was on its way to fall - but they sat with their feet tucked under their robes, hands clenched and plunged into pockets, and weren't bothered by the conditions. What impressed them most about that night was the rich fragrance of a newly mown lawn somewhere nearby.

"But even if we can't find our way back, at least we have a good friend in Dr. Holdsworth. He understands us and won't exploit us. A lot of men in Dr. Holdsworth's position would try to use our abilities for their personal gain."

"Like Spaulding, Rogers, and Brewer," Puu said. Bni nodded. What they were saying was nothing they hadn't gone over many times already. A squirrel poked its head inquisitively into the bush. Bni absently granted it the power

of flight. It gave an excited squeak, and flew off into a tree.

"Bni, you really shouldn't keep doing that," Puu *admonished mildly.*

"Why not?"

"Well, because. Squirrels weren't meant to fly. You're tampering with nature."

"Tampering with nature is the name of the game when you're a sorcerer, Buddy Boy," Bni *reminded him.* Puu *sighed.*

"You know, I really hate when you call me Buddy Boy," he *complained.*

"I hate that, too," Cozlu *said.* Then he *frowned. Tempers were getting short. He knew they'd have to return to their own time, or else...well, they just had to.*

"Hey, if we don't leave now we're going to be late," he *said abruptly, extending his arm to reveal the watch Dr. Holdsworth had given him. The other sorcerers studied the watch with him, then nodded in relief. The argument was put on hold. Silently, they moved off into the night, heading for the site of* The Great Book.

CHAPTER ONE

Now I'm not going to say that those foolish stones kept us from being seen by our enemies. I will say, however, that all five of us successfully made it to my apartment without incident. Myrna was out, and the place was cleaner than I'd ever seen it. Locking the door behind us, I pulled down all the shades, then confronted the others with a look that said, "Okay. Now what."

Scott asked Dr. Holdsworth where we should begin to dig. I winced. I still hadn't completely gotten used to the idea of digging up my kitchen floor. Obviously I didn't own the apartment, I just rented. I wasn't sure how I was going to explain the hole to my landlord. Maybe I'd tell him that some sorcerers were responsible: "They broke in while I was staying with a friend," I'd say. Meanwhile, Dr. Holdsworth had indicated a spot on the floor, which he marked off with a pencil.

"Wendy, your apartment is very unusual in that it's built on a foundation without a basement. All we have to do is dig through the floor, and we should find it," he told us. We nodded. It was amazing to think that he could narrow it down to one small square like that. I hoped the book would be there. But realistically, what were our chances of finding it? Pretty slim, if you ask me. Luckily, no one asked me. I got out the sharpest knife I owned, and handed it to Scott. Carefully, he sliced through the linoleum, along the lines that Dr. Holdsworth had drawn. I held my breath, as if I were watching an incision being made on my own body. Then I shrugged and relaxed. It was something that had to be done.

Just as Scott was tugging off the square of floor, a bright flash of light appeared, making us squint. We opened our eyes wide again as soon as we could, and to our astonishment, we discovered we'd been joined by three tiny men. Everyone gasped - we at them, and they at us. Even Dr. Holdsworth and Benjamin gasped, and they really didn't have any reason to, I mean, they already knew everyone there. But I guess they just got caught up in all the gasping.

Regally, the three sorcerers went over to Dr. Holdsworth, and greeted him solemnly. Scott, the only one who was seeing them for the first time, muttered, "Shit!" and glanced at me in disbelief. The sorcerers smiled when they noticed Benjamin, and to our amusement, he and Bni swapped Peace signs. It was very strange for me to be finally seeing them when I was awake. And they were so tiny! I suppose it shouldn't have surprised me. I mean, you go to any historical home, and you notice that the doorways and the ceilings are lower, and someone says, "Of course people were shorter then." And according to Dr. Holdsworth, these sorcerers had come from a time 3000 years ago. Kind of made you wonder how tall Adam and Eve had been. Kind of made you wonder if they'd been about the size of Ken and Barbie.

"Aren't they *darling*!" Delores cooed, crouching down the way adults do to children, and reaching out her hand. The sorcerers nodded politely, but didn't look at her. They were standing very close to Dr. Holdsworth, as if they were uncomfortable with so many strangers around. After a moment, he presented them, one by one. We all said, "Hello," and they said, "Hello" too, in tiny little voices. Then they turned to look at the exposed square of wood on the floor, apparently anxious to get to work. I couldn't take my eyes off them. I would have given a year of my life to touch them, just to assure myself that they were actually standing before me. Before us all. I glanced at Scott, and saw that he was smiling in awe and kind of shaking his head.

"Wowie," he said, and for some reason, it struck those of us from the 20th century as being pretty funny. We all laughed. The sorcerers exchanged bewildered looks; then, when they noticed that Dr. Holdsworth was laughing, they laughed, too. And for a minute, all of us laughed heartily, not because anything was particularly humorous, but because it felt so good to be laughing together. Then Dr. Holdsworth rubbed his hands together and suggested that we get started.

Scott hoisted the shovel he'd brought, and began to dig.

"How long do you think this will take?" Cozlu asked in his delicate voice. I noticed that he kept glancing at his watch. He'd stretch out his arm to pull back the sleeve of his robe, then he'd bend his elbow to look at the time. It was the gesture of a modern businessman that amused me. I wondered if the watch would survive the trip back, and what his friends would think of it.

"Not sure," Scott was saying. He was hacking away at the wood, but it was hard, and he just kept putting deep nicks into it. Then all at once he jammed his thumb painfully on the handle of the shovel.

"Aaaah, shit!" he cried, dropping the shovel and cradling the injured party of his right hand in his left hand.

"Scott, are you okay?" I asked, moving toward him. Delores, who, don't forget, was a nurse, asked to see the thumb, and gently moved it from side to side. From the look on poor Scott's face, it hurt like hell.

"Stop it, stop it," he said, trying to pull away.

"I hate to say this, but it's broken," Delores told him regretfully. We all said, "Oh no!" and circled around him, trying to comfort him, and staring at the thumb, which was starting to swell and turn red. He was holding it gingerly.

"Shit!" he said again.

"You should go get it set," Delores added.

"What, now? I'm busy now!" It was the first time I'd ever seen him upset. What a bitch, to have to stop digging and go to a hospital for medical attention. Probably going to cost him a couple of bucks, too. But it was the only thing he could do. He was really in pain. I patted his shoulder and smiled as if to say, "Oh well, these things happen," but for once he didn't smile back.

"Wait," said a tiny voice suddenly, "let us look at the thumb."

We turned to stare at the sorcerers. It was Puu who'd spoken, and he and the others were moving toward us. Scott sent me a questioning glance, then shrugged and knelt down and cautiously held out his hand. Cozlu, Puu, and Bni gathered around it, studied it without touching it, then nodded.

"Give us a second," Bni said. Scott said, "Sure," and waited patiently. The sorcerers spoke quietly among themselves for several moments in a language none of us recognized. Then, very gently, Cozlu put his tiny hand on Scott's swollen thumb. Bni murmured something in a melodious voice, and Puu reached into his pocket and withdrew a vial of powder, which he sprinkled on Scott's thumb. Scott started to say, "What the hell?" but stopped before he finished, and all at once his face lit up with wonder.

"Hey!" he said.

"What is it?" we all demanded.

"My thumb! It's healed!" And sure enough, when he held it up, we saw that the swelling had disappeared and that it was no longer red. Painlessly, he moved the thumb back and forth. None of us could believe our eyes. We all turned and stared in admiration at the sorcerers.

"Little trick of the trade," Bni explained casually, but he was pleased.

"Guess I'll go back to digging, then," Scott said cheerily, picking up the shovel and resuming his work.

I felt Delores touch my arm, and she whispered, "I'm sure his thumb was broken. I felt it! I can't understand how..." her voice faded, and she didn't say anything more. I just chuckled and shrugged.

Scott kept digging. We watched in silence for a little while. I think that for some reason we were all assuming that there would be dirt beneath the wood floor; then, under a couple of inches of dirt, we'd find the book, nestled safely in time. Imagine our dismay when Scott finally made it through the wood, and we heard the CLINK! of the shovel hitting cement.

"Oh pooh!" Delores voiced everyone's frustration. "Will your shovel be able to dig through cement?"

Scott frowned and didn't answer. He'd begun to sweat. With the back of his wrist, he wiped his forehead.

"Lemme take over for a while," Benjamin offered. Scott gladly relinquished the shovel, then came over to stand next to me.

"Doubt it," he finally told Delores.   We watched

Benjamin. The shovel was making a dent in the cement, but it wasn't exactly tearing it to pieces. I estimated that it would take about 3000 more years to break through the foundation. Benjamin must have realized that, too, because he stopped trying after only a few minutes and said we needed something more powerful.

"Like a jack hammer?" Scott asked.

"Good idea," I said wryly, "A jack hammer."

"Well, maybe not," he said, "but what should we do, then? There's no way this little ass shovel is going to-"

"Hey," I interrupted, "what about the sorcerers?"

We all turned to look at them. Already they'd begun to confer on the point. Cozlu reached for the shovel, which Benjamin willingly handed to him. He and Puu and Bni hovered over it for a moment, once again murmuring in that strange, melodious language. Bni pulled a vial out of his robe pocket, poured a drop of liquid on the shovel, and there was more chanting. Then Cozlu returned the shovel to Benjamin.

"This shovel now has the power to cut through cement as if it were cheese."

We non-sorcerers couldn't help chuckling. But we believed it. And sure enough, Benjamin took the shovel, positioned it on the section of cement that was visible, and with his foot, sank the shovel through the entire layer.

"I'll be damned!" he said. Effortlessly, he began to dig out the cement. We watched, fascinated. The sorcerers exchanged triumphant glances. Within a couple of minutes, Benjamin hit dirt. He told us merrily that it was like shoveling powder. Before we knew it, he'd dug a hole nearly three feet deep.

"We should be coming upon the book any time now," Dr. Holdsworth commented, consulting some notes he'd made.

We waited breathlessly. Yet still Benjamin continued to dig. After a little while, Scott took over. He, too, was amazed at the ease with which the shovel cut through the dirt. But no book appeared.

"Just a little deeper," Cozlu begged when Scott showed signs of abandoning the project. So Scott dug a foot or so deeper, then a foot deeper than that. By now a kind of desperate resignation had begun to settle over us all. I looked around at my apartment, appalled at how filthy and torn apart it was. The hole was no longer the size of Dr. Holdsworth's neat little square. It had reached a diameter of about two and a half feet. Scott was standing in a hole nearly five feet deep. Finally and dismally, we agreed it was time to give up. I helped Scott climb out.

"Someone must have found it and moved it," he said, "I'm really sorry."

The sorcerers were too devastated to even thank him for all his help. They looked miserably at one another. We all exchanged helpless looks. We wanted so badly to help them return to their own time.

"Don't worry, we'll think of something," Dr. Holdsworth tried to console them. He knelt before them and patted their little shoulders. I heard Delores sniff.

"Guess we should try to fill this in," Benjamin said, reaching for the shovel. He and Scott started replacing the dirt. Then they put the cement back in place, even though it was all in pieces. I began to wonder what the hell I was going to tell my landlord. The rest of us helped them gather up the wood chips, and we put those in the hole, too. Delores fetched a broom and swept everything in. And then they tried to cover it with the pieces of linoleum. But you can imagine what it looked like. There was a huge hole in my kitchen floor which was full of dirt, cement, and wood chips.

"Looks just like new," I said sarcastically, and then to my horror, I burst into tears. I couldn't help it. The sorcerers couldn't go back to their own time, I was going to have to pay a bundle to get the floor fixed, no one wanted to publish me, and I wasn't going to be able to finish Blake's assignment to tear apart Scott's article because I'd fallen in love with him and I wasn't sure if I could get him to love me back. The combination of all of these tragedies made me sob like a child. The others were amazed, and clustered around me.

"Don't worry, Wendy," Delores soothed, "everything's going to be fine."

"Oh yeah?" I challenged her, and we all looked at her as if to say, "How? How is everything going to be fine?"

"Don't sweat it, baby," we heard Bni say in a very kind voice. He and Cozlu and Puu gathered together into a triangle. Of course! I thought, The sorcerers can take care of it! I stopped crying, and as we watched, the three of them stretched out on the floor, covering the hole with their long robes. Puu had some powder which he applied liberally to their hands. Slowly, they pressed their fingers against the floor. Bni chanted quietly.

"That should do it," Puu said.

They rose slowly to their feet. And we saw to our delight and relief that the floor was once again perfectly intact. It was incredible! I dropped to my knees to test it. It was solid. I tried to thank the sorcerers, but they ducked their heads shyly and said that it had been nothing, that it was the least they could do.

"Jesus," Benjamin said.

"But Dr. Holdsworth, how will we be able to go back home?" Bni asked, and his face was full of sadness, and he heaved a little sigh. I felt so sorry for them all that I almost started to cry again. Dr. Holdsworth shrugged grimly.

After a moment, Scott asked, "What's the name of the book, anyway?"

"It's called *The Great Book of Spells, Rituals, and So On*," answered Cozlu miserably.

Scott's eyes flew open. Mine did, too.

"Are you serious?" Scott said.

"Of course. Why?"

"*The Great Book of Spells, Rituals, and So On*?" I repeated, just to make sure we'd heard him correctly.

"Yes. Why?"

"*The Great Book of Spells, Rituals, and So On* was on the Best Sellers List last year!" Scott shouted.

"Some guy in England just made a musical out of it!" I shouted, too.

"What? Are you sure?" the others demanded breathlessly.

"Yes! Yes!" Scott and I said, and we were giggling like fools.

"You mean to say that we can just go to a bookstore and buy it?" Benjamin wanted to know. "After all this digging?"

"My store doesn't carry it anymore," Scott said, "but some other places may still."

"Is it possible...are you sure it's the same book?" Dr. Holdsworth asked in amazement.

"Anything is possible," I said. Our disappointment and anxiety fizzled out and we all burst out laughing because it was so utterly ludicrous.

Then Cozlu glanced at his watch and said, "What time do the stores open?"

We all looked at the window and noticed for the first time that the sun had begun to come up.

"Pretty soon," I said. "Hey, let's go out and get some breakfast while we wait."

This was generally agreed upon; we all realized we were starving. We told the sorcerers we'd bring something back for them, and headed happily for the door, still chuckling and shaking our heads and saying, "Can you believe this? I can't believe this." But all at once the door flew open and Myrna came running in.

"Those horrible men kept me tied up all night! They took away my amulet, and kept asking me where the sorcerers were!" she wailed.

"Mother! Did they hurt you?" Benjamin asked, wrapping his arms around her protectively.

"No, Benjamin, I'm fine. I just kept telling them that I didn't know, and they had no choice but to believe me."

"So they let you go?"

"Heavens, no. They finally fell asleep. I kept working on the knots, and eventually got myself free, and ran off. But I'm sure that once they discover I'm gone this is the first place they'll come to look for me."

"Well we're just leaving," Scott said tersely, and he opened the door. But he slammed it shut right away. "Shit! They're here! Wendy - there a back door to this place?"

I nodded, and we hurried toward it. But we'd no sooner yanked it open than Brewer's horrible face appeared.

"Back this way!" I cried, and we headed toward the front door. At the same moment, it flew open, and there stood Spaulding and Rogers. They both had guns.

"Got you at last," sneered Spaulding.

We huddled together in a frightened clump, our eyes fastened on the guns menacingly pointed our way. I gripped Scott's hand and said, "Shit, Scott! What do we do now?"

"You give us the book, that's what you do," roared Brewer, "Or else we'll kill you one by one. And we're gonna start with you!"

As he yanked me away from Scott, the thought, What have I done with my life? tore cruelly through my mind. I realized I'd done nothing...nothing but criticize the world! And wasn't that even worse than nothing? My God, I thought, I've been healthy and I've had enough to eat and a place to live and I've made a lot of friends, and I had every opportunity to be happy, and to spread that happiness, but I didn't. I thought it was more sophisticated to be miserable. I thought it was impossible to be happy when the world was so fucked up. But I could have been! I could have been, and now it's too late!

Suddenly, and to the surprise of everyone, that feisty old Myrna sank her uncared for teeth into Brewer's hand. With a howl, he retracted it. Then he grabbed her by the neck and slammed her hard against the wall. We heard something go CRACK! and poor Myrna crumpled to the floor.

"Myrna!" I dropped to my knees and took her face in my hands.

"Mother!" Benjamin cried painfully, kneeling beside me. Delores knelt, too, and checked Myrna's vital signs. Meanwhile, Myrna struggled to speak. She choked a little, and with the first words, blood dribbled out the side of her mouth.

"My amulet," she whispered, feebly feeling her neck for it. "It's gone. That means I'm going to die."

"No, Mother!" Benjamin cried. He pulled her head onto his lap, and began to stroke her forehead. I saw she was bleeding from the ear, and that part of her face was crushed in. We could tell she wasn't going to make it. "Here,"

Benjamin said suddenly, starting to pull off his amulet, "take mine!"

"No," she stopped him in a voice so quiet we had to lean in close to hear her. "They made that for you, it's only good for you."

"I'll get yours, then!" I said, starting to scramble to my feet. But Delores pulled me back and said that there wasn't time. I looked back at Myrna and saw that she was smiling at me.

"Wendy," she said.

"What." I was at her side in a second, and took her cold little hand in mine.

Her breath was coming in spurts. She had to pause in between words as she said, "I want...you to...keep in mind every...thing I've...told you...about...opening...up...your mind."

"I will, I will," I promised her earnestly.

"Good girl," she said. And then with a tiny sigh, she died. Just like that. Her eyes, still gazing at my face, lost their focus, but remained open. Delores gently shut them, then checked for a heartbeat. There was none. So she shook her head. Then she looked up at Brewer with a hate filled glare.

"She's dead. And you killed her."

I stared at Delores in reluctant surprise. I thought, No, Myrna can't be dead! She was fine a minute ago! and I waited for someone to say, "No, she isn't dead after all." But no one did. Benjamin laid his head on his mother's chest and began to weep quietly. We heard him apologize for not giving her a better life, for not supporting her and giving her a nice home to live in. I leaned back a little and saw that my hands were shaking violently. Scott knelt beside me and pulled me close. The thugs watched us, silent, undecided if they should be ashamed or not.

"She tried to help me," I said, dazed.

"She did. She did help you," Scott said.

"She tried to help me in my last life, too," I went on, and my voice sounded odd to me, fragile and far away. Scott didn't respond, he just patted my arm and let me go on. "I was so rude to her the first time we met. I didn't even know her, and I assumed she was ignorant and crazy."

"But then you were kind to her. You let her stay in your apartment," Scott reminded me gently.

I tore my eyes off Myrna and looked at him sorrowfully.

"Why am I always like that? Why am I so quick to judge? She tried to warn me, and I didn't even thank her! She died for me, and I never even got to tell her how grateful I am. God! If only I could speak to her just one more time and let her know!"

The moment the words left my mouth I thought, Wait! The sorcerers can save her! I raised my tear filled eyes to them.

"Can you do it?" I whispered desperately. Benjamin looked up, too. "Can you bring her back?"

Every eye in the room was on the three tiny, bashful sorcerers. Spaulding, Brewer, and Rogers, who hadn't even noticed them before, gasped in disbelief. Cozlu, Puu, and Bni exchanged uncomfortable glances, each waiting for the other to speak. And finally Cozlu coughed nervously and shook his head.

"I'm sorry, but no, we can't. You see, Myrna had karmic obligations in this life, and she's just fulfilled them. You saved her from harm in a past life, and she chose to return the favor in this life. It was the only way she could advance to become a more spiritually evolved soul. If we were to bring her back to life, it would just foul everything up."

"What are you talking about?" Delores demanded, looking from one face to the other, feeling as if she was the only one there who didn't understand.

"The Divine Plan," Benjamin conceded regretfully. "We choose our destinies. Mother chose this one. Cozlu is right. We can't fuck with it."

"So we should be happy for her," Scott said, and he even managed to smile. "She's released herself from the earthly bonds that held her to you. She can dedicate her next life to her own growth. She'll be much happier."

"I'm going to miss her, though," Benjamin said sadly.

"We all will," I said, pulling him toward me and giving him a hug. "She was a very good woman."

Benjamin nodded but didn't answer. He was too overcome. Fleetingly, I wondered how I was going to explain Myrna's body to my landlord.

"Enough of this," Spaulding spoke up suddenly in a voice so nasty it made my skin crawl. "It's been a touching scene, but now it's time to give us that book. Because if you don't, you'll *all* be released from your 'earthly bonds!'"

CHAPTER TWO

"We don't have the book," Dr. Holdsworth announced, spreading his empty hands apart in a gesture that correlated with this lack. Rogers startled us by leaping forward, seizing Dr. Holdsworth by the collar, and slamming him violently against the wall.

"Look!" he exploded, "I've had enough of your shit! Now tell us where the fucking book is, or I'll crush your skull!"

"I told you, we don't have it," Dr. Holdsworth whimpered, squirming and looking at the rest of us frantically.

Scott stepped forward very bravely and advised in his gentle voice, "Let him go. He's telling the truth - we don't have the book. But we know where to get it."

The thugs turned to Scott with interest. Rogers released Dr. Holdsworth with a vindictive little shake.

"Well? Where is it?" Brewer demanded. The three of them were really ugly, with thick necks and bad complexions, tiny, mean eyes, and receding hair lines. Looking at them made me a little sick to my stomach.

"It seems that Dr. Holdsworth made an error in his calculations," Scott went on, "The book is buried beneath a

179

building up the street."

"You're lying!" Rogers roared, lunging toward Scott. But Scott stood his ground, wearing a benevolent, even helpful smile on his face. Rogers stopped short of him, then glanced back at Spaulding and Brewer.

"Let's search them for the book," Spaulding suggested.

So we were all subject to an impromptu body search, particularly Delores and me. Those horrible thugs ran their hands up and down our bodies, sneering, "Is this the book? What's this? Is this the book?" and grabbing us in places we'd rather not be grabbed in. All in all, it was very humiliating. I was in a real rage by the time they finally determined that we didn't have the book anywhere on us.

"See? Told you," Scott said.

"Hey!" Brewer said suddenly, "Where'd those little guys go?"

For the first time, we realized that the sorcerers had disappeared.

"Shouting upsets them," Dr. Holdsworth said.

The thugs glared at us. Then Spaulding shoved his terrible face in Scott's sweet gentle one and said, "Alright, Mr. Smart Ass, suppose you tell us where the book is."

"Up the street. Here - let me get my shovel and we'll go look for it."

The three thugs traded doubtful glances. I could tell they were trying to decide whether or not Scott was telling the truth. The last time they'd accused him of being a liar, he'd proven that he was being honest with them. They just didn't know what to think. In the meantime, Scott had picked up the shovel and was heading for the door. In a flash, I was right behind him.

"Coming?" he asked.

The thugs nodded, and we all filed out the door and began to walk up the street. I wanted to ask Scott where he was taking us, but I didn't dare. So I kept quiet and wondered what had become of the sorcerers. I supposed they had simply dematerialized. Dr. Holdsworth had said they could do that.

We walked for several minutes. Scott led us with such a purposeful stride that I knew he had a specific location in mind. As for the rest of us - Dr. Holdsworth, Benjamin, Delores and me - we all concentrated on keeping our expressions confident, like, "Sure, we know exactly where we're going," as, filled with doubt and fear, we followed Scott. He was saying, "It turned out that Dr. Holdsworth forgot to take into consideration a couple of leap years, and that threw the calculations off. The site we'd originally planned to dig in turned out to be a mile or so off the mark. Luckily, he realized it before we started to dig up Wendy's floor. Just before you guys showed up, he went over his numbers again, and determined that the book is buried right here, beneath this police station."

Abruptly, Scott came to a halt. We did, too, each one bumping into the one ahead of him. Then we looked up, and sure enough, we were standing in front of a police station.

"So let's go inside!" Scott said merrily, grabbing me and dashing up the stairs. Delores grabbed Dr. Holdsworth, and Dr. Holdsworth grabbed Benjamin, who was in kind of a daze. And then all five of us hurried inside. Back on the sidewalk, Spaulding, Brewer, and Rogers hunched their faces into their shoulders and took off. We burst out laughing.

"Help you?" a voice behind us inquired.

We spun around and saw about half a dozen officers staring at us in curiosity.

"Um, I think not." Dr. Holdsworth said. Delores flashed

her nifty smile, and Scott said "Thanks, anyway."

We hurried back out, and ran off in the opposite direction the thugs had gone.

"I've seen it at the B.U. bookstore," Scott said, and so we went there. He knew exactly where it was. Taking a copy from the shelf, he handed it triumphantly to Dr. Holdsworth. We saw that it was an innocent looking book, bright blue with yellow letters that said, *The Great Book of Spells, Rituals, and So On.* It was a little eerie to be looking at it, after having dug up my kitchen floor in search of it the night previous. Dr. Holdsworth flipped through the pages, and peering over his shoulder we saw that sure enough, it contained spells. Like a cookbook filled with recipes. I wondered how the guy in England was going to turn it into a musical.

"Okay, let's get our friends on their way," Dr. Holdsworth said with a sentimental smile. He paid for the book, then we headed out. With heads turning this way and that, we determined that the thugs were nowhere in sight.

"But Dr. Holdsworth," Delores said after a moment, "How come they saw us? I thought you said with those stones-"

"There must have been some unbelievers present," Dr. Holdsworth murmured. He means me, I thought, hot with guilt.

"You really think that's all it takes," I said, "faith?"

"That's all," he said.

"But," I said, "how can a person genuinely have faith in powers he's been conditioned his whole life to believe don't exist? I mean, I've never, not in twenty eight years, been told that if I carry a certain type of stone I can avoid being seen. Honest - last night was the first time. Now I'm not saying that this faith business is a bad thing. My point is, it seems like it's almost impossible to cultivate it in this society."

"Almost impossible," Dr. Holdsworth concurred.

Scott interrupted suddenly to suggest that we take his car to Delores' house instead of going back to my place, where the thugs were sure to find us. We agreed that that would best, and headed off in that direction.

"But Dr. Holdsworth," I wanted to resume the discussion on faith, "I can't make a thing true simply be convincing myself that it's true. Can I?"

"Why not?"

"What do you mean, why not! I just can't! I can't convince myself that the city of Boston no longer exists, and have it be true!"

"If you could convince yourself that Boston no longer existed, then you would no longer see it, which means it would no longer exist to you. Of course other people would have a different perception of the city. To them, it would still be the same as it always was."

"Sure, Wendy," Scott put in, "It's like all those people who are convinced they're the Messiah."

"Yes, but they're not really the Messiah. They just think they are."

"What's the difference?"

I didn't answer. I was trying to take it all in. I couldn't help it, I just couldn't buy it.

"Wendy, have you ever read the Bible?" Dr. Holdsworth asked suddenly.

"The Bible?"

"Yeah, you know, black cover, pages with gold edges..."

"I've started it a couple of times," I said, "but I can never finish it. God comes across as such a pompous, vindictive fool, wanting to be praised all the time and instilling a terrible fear in the hearts of man. And we're still under the influence of that fear. Go to any Catholic ceremony and you'll be urged to fear God. And I mean, what's the sense in that?"

"I agree with you on that point," Dr. Holdsworth said, "I think that over the years we've gotten farther and farther away from the original message of the Bible. We've concentrated on the negative aspects of it - don't do this, don't do that - and we never heed the positive advice. All over the world there are millions of people who think they're living good, Christian lives, because they're not killing anyone or coveting their neighbor's wife. But unless they give of themselves, they're missing the boat. I like to regard the Bible as a novel that's supposed to leave you thinking. Like a book by Dostoyevsky. He taught us that there can be good in every man, even convicts in a prison. That, to me, is a worthwhile message."

"Well, we seem to have digressed a bit," I said. I've always admired Dostoyevsky for his portrayal of the pathetic, ineffective Underground Man, and even though I've heard him referred to as a Christian, I never think of him that way.

"You're right. Well, I was going to ask you if you'd read about the woman in the New Testament who'd been bleeding for years and years. She'd gone to several doctors, but none could help her. Finally, when Jesus came to town, she decided that if she could just touch His robe, she would be healed. So she pushed her way through the crowd, bent down, and touched the fabric. And sure enough, she was instantly healed! But it wasn't Jesus who healed her, or even His robe. It was her faith. And I think that was Jesus' message: We all have his power. We're all Jesus, we're all wearing His robe. We just don't realize it."

I said, "Oh," and fell silent. No one else said anything either. We were all thinking about what Dr. Holdsworth had said. I vaguely recalled reading the story about the bleeding woman, but hadn't given it any thought at the time. But now I was really pondering the whole thing. Was I to understand that if I believed I could do anything, then I *could* do anything? It sounded so trite! Could a cliché actually be the meaning of life? Well...why not?

At that moment, I felt something inside give way, like a wall crumbling, and I decided to believe it all. I mean, I doubted that I would ever be able to make it rain, or talk to animals, but that was because I had no desire to do those things. All I wanted to do was write, and affect people with my writing. Up until that point I'd always considered it my duty as a writer to make everyone see that the world was full of crooks and weasels. But suddenly I realized there really wasn't much sense in that. Suddenly I thought that maybe I should use my writing to encourage people to try to make things better.

Well as soon as that realization hit me, I felt my face light up, like I'd just come across a valuable coin lying in the road. I looked around at the others, thinking for sure they'd seen the transformation on my face. But none had. Each was buried in his or her own thoughts. So I kept the revelation to myself. But at that moment, my outlook changed. Sometimes that's the way it happens, all at once like that.

Before I knew it, we'd reached Scott's car. With apprehensive glances all around, we piled in and took off, headed for Delores' house. It suddenly occurred to me that the sorcerers probably didn't know where Delores lived. But as if I'd voiced the remark out loud, Dr. Holdsworth said confidently, "They'll know where to find us."

"But how? They've never been there."

"They've become susceptible to my vibrations," Dr.

Holdsworth explained.   None of us said anything for a moment, and then we all nodded.   Like him, we were confident they'd find their way to us somehow.

Sure enough, we'd no sooner arrived than we were joined by them; once again they made their entrance with a brilliant flash of light that made us blink our eyes in amazement.

"Did you get it? Did you get it?" they demanded all at once.   With a big, fatherly grin, Dr. Holdsworth held it up. Three sets of magnificent blue eyes fastened on it, three wrinkled old faces lit up.   It was a pleasure to watch them dance in glee around Dr. Holdsworth's legs.   I felt fortunate to witness it.   And I realized I would never forget the moment, or feel the same way again.   I looked over at Scott and saw that he was smiling at me.   Reaching out, he took my hand and gave it a squeeze.

"Let's see it, let's see it!" clamored the sorcerers.   He said, "Hold on," in an affectionate voice, and herded them toward the house.   Delores unlocked the door and let us in. And finally, he handed it to them.

They took it wordlessly, reverently.

"But, how is it that this book is sold to just anyone?" Puu asked, and his little face was lined with bewilderment.   "In our time it was esoteric, and forbidden to all but a very few.   But now that anyone has access to it, why aren't people using it? Why are there still wars and poverty and illness?"

"Because these spells can only be performed by those who believe in magic," Dr. Holdsworth answered, "and very few people today believe in magic."

"Like raising the Pentagon," Bni said suddenly, thoughtfully focusing his steady gaze on Benjamin.

"Exactly," said Benjamin.

The rest of us exchanged looks that said, "What?" and

waited for an explanation. Bni was too bashful to speak for any significant length of time, so Benjamin began.

"It was 1967. The Summer of Love, and all that. Uppermost in the minds of the young people that year was the war in Vietnam. Everyone I knew was opposed to it - we all protested it and burned our draft cards. But it wasn't enough. So a bunch of us came up with this idea to descend upon the Pentagon, and try to exorcise the demons who lived there. See, the Pentagon is the mind of the country, and we felt that if we could free it of the evil within, then we, the body, would be a lot better off. So we told everyone that we were going to levitate the Pentagon, make it spin around, and turn orange. I know it sounds bizarre," he chuckled, seeing the looks on our faces, "but originally it was just a concept, you know, just a kind of project that would involve all of us. I mean, we didn't really think we could lift a building off its foundation. But then some guys from California showed up and said, 'Count us in.' It seemed that one of them had been consulting with someone in Mexico who claimed it really could be done. I mean, these guys from the West Coast were convinced we could do it. So we marched to Washington, gathered around the Pentagon, and recited all kinds of chants. We generated a powerful energy, based solely on our faith. We knew we'd be able to make it leave the ground."

Benjamin paused. He was no longer with us, he was back in Washington D.C, and it was about 25 years ago. I glanced at Bni and saw that he was completely captivated by Benjamin's story.

"Well so what happened?" Scott asked impatiently.

"We raised it. About 3:00 in the morning it went up. It didn't go very far, and it didn't spin or turn orange. But it went up. I saw it. My girlfriend saw it. And Abbie Hoffman saw it. We raised the Pentagon because we *believed* we could."

We were all dead silent for several minutes, trying to imagine what that must have been like. It must have been an incredibly sight, like the launching of a space shuttle. I noticed that the others were kind of nodding, and then I realized that I was nodding, too. "Well, let's get this show on the road," Scott grinned. We all grinned back and said, "Yes, let's!" But then Dr. Holdsworth held up his hand for silence.

"Wait," he said.

"What," we said together, thinking he was going to say there was a problem.

But he didn't say anything like that. On the contrary. Facing the sorcerers, he said, "Would it be okay if I went back in time with you? If I stay here, I'll never be able to escape from Spaulding, Brewer, and Rogers. They'll follow me everywhere for the rest of my life, always hounding me for the secret that will enable them to rule the world."

"You want to go back in time with us?" Bni said in amazement.

"It's all I can think about. Ever since this whole thing started, I've known what I wanted to do. If it's okay with you." Anxiously, he awaited their answer. They looked at one another, then nodded.

"Of course you can come with us," Cozlu said warmly.

"Really? I can?" Dr. Holdsworth said, and he wore a big grin like a kid who's been excused from school for the rest of his life.

"But Dr. Holdsworth," I said, "what about all the information you've learned from the sorcerers? Are you going to take it back with you, and not share it with anyone?"

Dr. Holdsworth reached into his pocket, withdrew his

wallet, and pulled out a key, which he gave to me.

"This opens a locker down at South Station where I've put written transcripts of everything the sorcerers have told me. I want you to go through it and present it to the world in your own way. Maybe you can turn it into a novel. Maybe it will get your writing career off the ground. Don't you think it's time you concentrated on doing some good with your gift?"

"Yes," I said, "I do."

I took the key and dropped it into my purse. Scott beamed at me. Dr. Holdsworth took a moment to hug Delores and me, then shook hands with Scott and Benjamin.

"Okay," he said, going over to stand next to the sorcerers, "let's go!"

CHAPTER THREE

For as long as I live, I'll never forget the look on the faces of the three sorcerers when Dr. Holdsworth said those words. They glanced nervously at one another, and their happy faces clouded over.

"I hate to say this," Cozlu began.

"What? What?" Dr. Holdsworth demanded.

"Well, we can't go back yet."

There was a stunned silence. Then Dr. Holdsworth quietly asked why not.

"Because it's the middle of the day. This spell has to be done just before dawn. Really! See? It says so right here in the book: 'This spell must be performed in the final hours of the night.' I'm sorry. But it's true."

Well talk about anticlimactic. We were all simply flabbergasted. No one could even speak for a few minutes. As for the sorcerers, they stared down at their wrinkled, old hands, sheepish, regretful, and a little ashamed.

"What happens if you do the spell in the middle of the day?" Scott asked finally. We all nodded as if to say, "Yes, what if?" But the sorcerers shook their heads firmly.

"Disaster," Cozlu said forebodingly.

"Disaster?" Scott echoed.

"Yes."

"What kind of disaster?"

"Who cares what kind of disaster," groaned Puu, "Disaster is disaster."

"But are you sure?"

All three sorcerers heaved giant sighs at once. Clearly this wasn't easy for them, and Scott was making it even more difficult.

"You'll just have to take our word for it," Bni said.

"But why?" Scott persisted. "Have you ever known anyone to do this spell in the middle of the day?"

"No, but-"

"Then how do you know-"

"Because *The Great Book* says you're supposed to do it just before dawn! And we have to do whatever *The Great Book* says!"

"Well, why don't you just try it now? I mean, what's the worst that can happen?"

Dr. Holdsworth nodded. He was eager to get going, and waiting until the final hours of the night didn't appeal to him in the slightest. Not only that, the thugs could show up at any moment.

"Because *The Great Book-*"

"Fuck *The Great Book!*" Scott exploded; then added somewhat contritely, "I mean, that's the problem with you sorcerers. You're so willing to believe in your own powers that you wind up believing in other powers, too - powers that don't even exist. You can't place so much emphasis on words in a book. Don't you see? It's great to believe in some things, but to believe in everything can cripple you. It makes you superstitious, and fills you with needless fear. Hell, it seems to me that if you *really* believed in your powers, you

191

wouldn't even need *The Great Book.*"

There was an intense silence. The sorcerers were staring at Scott with their tiny jaws hanging slack. They'd just been advised to "Fuck *The Great Book,*" and you figure that had to have unnerved them just a bit. Still, they tried to decide if Scott had a valid point or not. It sounded logical...but the idea of not acting in accordance with the rules in *The Great Book* was something that had never occurred to them before. They'd had about 60 or 70 years of believing everything *The Great Book* said. The rest of us saw at once that Scott was absolutely right, that you can't believe everything you read. But it took the sorcerers a couple of minutes to collect themselves and ponder his advice. Finally Bni said in his sweet, melodious voice, "I can dig that. We have the ability to go back in time, no matter what the conditions. So let's toodle-oo."

Cozlu and Puu regarded him with surprise. Usually it was left to Cozlu to make the major decisions. However, he and Puu could not help but agree that it was certainly worth a shot.

"Okay," Cozlu said, and a moment later they were preparing themselves for the trip. Bni took the book, located the spell, and the other time travelers joined him in a small circle. Scott held my hand very tightly. He and Delores and Benjamin and I watched very carefully. Bni began to chant. The words were unfamiliar and mysterious. I tried to make sense out of them, but couldn't. Everyone was very solemn. Dr. Holdsworth's eyes were fastened on Bni's face as he read the spell. His voice was very pleasing, very soothing. Cozlu shut his eyes, and a tiny, content smile appeared on his face.

I don't know about anyone else, but after a moment of listening to Bni, I began to feel kind of funny...dizzy. I felt as if I could easily have dropped off to sleep, but of course I didn't want to. I didn't want to miss anything. Nevertheless, it was a real struggle to keep my eyes open. I felt like I was watching the whole scene from high in the air.

And suddenly the door burst open and in flew Spaulding, Rogers, and Brewer!

"On no!" Scott said, pulling me close. The three thugs exchanged triumphant grins, then turned questioningly to the scenario being played out in the middle of Delores' living room.

"How did you know where to find us?" Delores asked, dismayed. From his pocket Spaulding withdrew a copy of the newspaper where I'd first read about Delores' experience with the sorcerers near the Swan Boats.

"Wasn't too tough," he snarled.

"Why don't you just leave us alone," I said. By this time I was more annoyed than frightened. I mean, it was really getting ridiculous, them popping up every time we were all set to do something.

"Shut up!" Brewer said, and he was pissed. "Or I'll finish the job I started on you, and that old hag won't be around to save you."

He took a step closer. But Scott blocked his way. My hero, I thought admiringly.

"Wait," Bni said suddenly.

The thugs turned and stared.

"You talking to me?" Brewer asked.

"Yeah, you, man," Bni said cheerily. "I believe this is what you're looking for." He tossed him *The Great Book*. Brewer scrambled for it. "Everything you need to know to rule the world is in there."

"This?" Brewer asked skeptically. It sure looked like an

unlikely tool - brand new, bright blue, and a paperback to boot.

"The real power is within," Cozlu said.

"Believe in yourselves," Puu added.

"And stay cool!" Bni giggled. Then to our amazement there was a smokey explosion and a brilliant flash of light. We covered our faces and squeezed our eyes tightly shut. Scott held me close, and I could feel his heart thumping. I heard him mutter, "Holy shit!" and he released me. I looked around. Everyone was staring in awe at the spot where only seconds before Dr. Holdsworth had stood with a trio of sorcerers.

"They're gone!" Spaulding said, and there was wonder in his voice. "Brewer! Gimme that book!"

Wordlessly, Brewer brought it over to him. Spaulding excitedly began to look through it. Rogers joined them, and the three of them started reading it as quickly as possible.

"Look at this! Look at this! Spells to affect the weather! Spells to hypnotise people! Spells to predict the future! Do you guys know what this means? We can do anything!"

"Yeah, anything!" Rogers echoed, and with a joyful shout, they ran out the door.

"Why did Bni give them that book? Now they're going to take over the world!" Delores said.

"I wouldn't worry about it," Scott advised, and he was chuckling a little. "What those guys don't realize is that you can't use magic for diabolical purposes. There are stronger forces in the universe that prevent that kind of thing. Hey, I could sure use a beer. Got any?"

Delores nodded wordlessly, and disappeared to fetch one. When she returned with it, Scott cracked it open, sipped it, then passed it to me. I sipped it and passed it to Delores, who sipped it and passed it to Benjamin. We were all thinking hard. Scott was probably right. The thugs would go back to their shady headquarters, read through the spells, and give up when they met with only failure. Scott was definitely right. They didn't believe in themselves enough to perform magic; because if you truly believe in yourself, you have no desire to rule the world.

We finished up the beer, then Scott said we'd better get going.

"Can we drop you off anywhere, Benjamin?" he asked kindly. Then he said, "Shit! I mean, we have to do something about..."

"Oh yeah," I said, "Myrna is still in my apartment. What should we do with her?"

None of us knew. I got another beer from the refrigerator, and while we tried to come to some kind of decision, we finished that one, too.

"Maybe we could make it look like she was attacked on the street," I suggested. "Drag, I mean carry her out tonight, and put her somewhere..." My voice trailed off. What a horrible thought. What if this were my mother we were talking about? I realized I hadn't called my parents in a couple of weeks, and decided I'd take the time to go visit them as soon as I could.

"How about if we put her in your bed, and say she was staying there while you were staying with me, and that someone must have snuck in and..." Scott, too, stopped. We knew it was a story no detective in his right mind would buy.

"I wonder if we should just put Mother in the harbor or something," Benjamin sighed guiltily, but I shook my head right away.

"No - someone might see us carrying her out. Damn!"

"You know what I wish?" Scott said suddenly. "I wish that we'd go back to your place, Wendy, and that her body would be gone."

"Gone?" I repeated, "What do you mean?"

"Just what I said. I wish that we would get there and find that all evidence of her had disappeared."

He was staring at me with an intense, significant gleam in his eyes. At first, I didn't understand at all what he was getting at. I heard Delores say, "Scott, what are you talking about?" and then all at once I knew.

"You mean if we concentrate, and believe, we can sort of...dematerialize her?"

"Worth a try, isn't it?"

Benjamin and Delores gasped. But then we all thought, Sure, why not. So we sat down on the floor, shut our eyes, and for about twenty minutes, we concentrated hard and believed, and willed Myrna's body to disappear. I don't know what method the others used, but I performed a visualization exercise I leaned in some off-the-wall psychology course I'd taken in college. I pictured Myrna's body lying exactly as we left it. Then slowly and gradually and in great detail, I imagined it fading. I imagined her getting fainter and fainter. And when I'd completely erased her body from my mind, I opened my eyes and stretched luxuriously. The others were still concentrating. I saw that Benjamin was fingering the amulet the sorcerers had given him. I turned my attention to Scott. His face looked peaceful and relaxed. For the millionth time, I wondered if I was going to be able to get him to fall in love with me. He'd been very affectionate and protective of me, but maybe he was just acting out of friendship. If only I knew! Just then his eyes opened and met mine. We both smiled.

196

"All set?" he said. I nodded. Benjamin and Delores opened their eyes, and nodded, too. "Okay. Let's get going then. Delores, we'll call you from Wendy's and let you know how it went. Okay?"

Delores said, "Okay," and walked us to the door. There was a feeling of warmth and confidence. We all smiled calm smiles. I doubt that any of us were worried. We said goodbye to Delores, and climbed back into Scott's car.

The ride back to my place was quiet. I felt curiously refreshed. I felt like a lot of the anxiety I'd been carrying around for years and years had evaporated. Suddenly most of my problems seemed pretty trivial. My entire body felt relaxed; even my face felt relaxed. I felt like I probably looked about five years younger. It would have been very easy for me to drop off to sleep; I hadn't been sleeping well because of the nightmares, and instinctively, I knew they were gone for good. All at once I was filled with a wonderful sense of contentment that I hadn't felt since the days when I used to nap in the back seat of my parents' station wagon, listening to them talk, and not waking up until we reached home.

When we got back to my apartment, we climbed wordlessly out of the car. I let us in, and immediately our eyes flew to the place on the floor where we'd left Myrna. There was no sign of her. No sign at all.

"Well, that's that," I said. Impulsively, I reached out and hugged Benjamin very tightly.

"She knew that you loved her, and that's the most important thing in the world," I said.

"I know," he said.

"What will you do now?" Scott asked him. Benjamin shrugged.

"Not sure. Go find some place to live. Maybe get a

job."

"How about staying here?" Scott said, glancing at me. "I mean, if Wendy doesn't mind staying with me."

My eyes flew open; an incredible joy filled me. He wants me to stay with him! I thought. I'm going to do it! I'm going to make him fall in love with me!

"I don't mind," I said.

Benjamin grinned broadly.

"Really?"

"Of course."

Scott called Delores and reported that our spell had been successful. I heard him say he'd talk to her soon, then he hung up. We said goodbye to Benjamin, then got into Scott's car again. And before too long we were pulling up to his apartment. Our apartment.

"Hey Wendy," he said abruptly, turning off the engine, but not getting out. "Mind if I ask you something?"

"What."

"Remember when you showed up at my apartment that first night and told me about the sorcerers in your room?"

"Yes."

"Well, how did you know where I lived?"

I started to tell him that his address had been on the envelope Blake had given me, but luckily I stopped myself before I did. I didn't want him to know anything about my assignment to tear apart the article he'd submitted to *The No Frills Dirt*. So I took a deep breath and said, "Well for crying out loud, Scott, you must know that I've had a crush on you for months and months."

He was startled.

"What? No, I didn't know that! You have? But how? We haven't even known each other a week yet!"

"I know, but I've seen you in the bookstore and stuff," I mumbled. My face was bright red as I scrambled out of the car. He got out, too, and as we met at the curb, he took my hand.

"Well, I think that's sweet," he said.

Embarrassed and awkward, I ducked my head and plunged my other hand into the pocket of my jeans. My fingers encountered something hard and round.

"Hey, what's this?" I withdrew a white stone with a pitch black center. Belocolus. I held it out to Scott. "Prevents me from being seen," I said.

"I hope it won't prevent me from seeing you," he grinned.

It was kind of a corny thing to say, but it made me blush all over. And then he cupped my face in his hands and kissed me. I felt my insides sag with relief and bliss. I did it, I thought. And in a flash I pictured Scott and me years from now, married and teaching our kids all about believing in themselves and in the wonderful world we all live in.

CHAPTER FOUR

"Let's get ourselves a nice celebration dinner," Scott suggested, and so we walked past the diner we'd eaten at a few night ago, into an air conditioned, well lit restaurant, where we were seated by a smiling hostess.

Scott and I both ordered ice tea, and when it arrived, we clinked our glasses together in an unspoken toast. Then Scott remarked casually that he didn't have to go to work until late in the afternoon the following day. The look on his face said, "So I can stay up late tonight if I want to," and I felt a thrill shoot through me. I knew it was understood that after dinner we'd go home and make love. I'm the luckiest woman alive, I thought.

Over steaming hot linguini with vegetables and tomato sauce, I asked him to tell me about himself, if he had any brothers and sisters, what his parents were like, and that kind of thing.

"Well," he began, "I'm an only child. My parents were very population conscious. In fact, they tried to adopt, but there was such a long waiting list that they finally said, 'Well, we'll just have one.' So they had me.

"When I was real young, we lived on a small farm. We had a couple of chickens and a cow that was so irritable no one could milk her without getting kicked. Our neighbors told us to get rid of her, because none of us really liked the taste of her milk, but my parents always said-"

"Why did you milk her if you didn't like the milk?" I interrupted benightedly.

"Cows have to be milked, Wendy," Scott said, and he was smiling a little bit.

"Well how was I supposed to know," I said.

"When was the last time you saw a real live cow?"

"I have no idea. Why?"

"Well, I'm just thinking that maybe it's time you left the city and spent some time in the country. Next chance we get, let's go to Vermont and visit my parents. Then you'll be able to see some real nature. You'll be able to breath fresh air, and there won't be a zillion cars speeding past you, or garbage in the street, or-"

"Hold on a second," I said, "I can't just sit back and let you criticize Boston. I mean, sure, we've got a lot of problems. What city doesn't? The air stinks. It's filthy. Parts of it are dangerous. I know that. But look at what we've accomplished. We're on the cutting edge of technology, Scott. We've developed new types of medicine and we've helped send men to the moon. We've made advances in every field there is - science, medicine, arts, even sports. I mean, Scott! We've got the *Red Sox*!"

"What's your point," he said.

"My point is, sure, Vermont is a clean, fresh place. But what has Vermont done for me? Has Vermont forfeited any of its beauty to save my life? Or to improve my living conditions? When you were living in Vermont, you were using products manufactured here in Massachusetts every single day, Scott. So you have no right to sit back and brag about how unpolluted your state is. "

He was startled by my sudden indignation. I was a little surprised, too, if you want to know the truth. But I've always been proud of my heritage, and I don't care who knows it.

"Look," I went on, and my tone was gentler, "I'm not saying that my state is better than your state. I'm saying that they both have merit. Vermont sounds like a great get away, or a perfect place to live a good, simple, useful life. But here in Massachusetts, we innovate. We can't help ourselves. We're always looking for a better, less expensive, more effective way to do things. That's how we are. That's why we came here in the first place. Yeah, we fucked up our water. We have to live with that. But we have value, too, Scott. Just like Vermont."

I wasn't sure if he was pissed or not. I'd had no intention of attacking Vermont, because I hoped he would take there to see it soon. But I needed him to see my side of things, too. I didn't want him feeling sorry for me just because I hadn't seen a live cow in a long time.

"We have technology in Vermont," he said after a moment.

"I'm sure you do. And we have nature here in Massachusetts," I countered. At the same time, we both reached for our glasses of ice tea. We sipped together in silence.

And then he said, "You're right. Cities are ugly, but they're necessary. Likewise, the foliage in Vermont is the most beautiful in the world, but not particularly useful. I apologize."

He was so humble that I had to forgive him. Besides, I admired him for having a fierce pride in his home state, just the way I did. We swapped smiles. We'd disagreed, and we'd reached a compromise we were both satisfied with. Life with Scott is going to be great, I thought happily.

"I'm done eating," he said. "Are you?"

I said I was. So he motioned the waitress over, and paid her. I thanked him guiltily. I suddenly realized that he'd done nothing but pamper me every since I showed up at his door in the middle of the night. We walked back to his apartment in silence, holding hands. It was a beautiful summer evening, with a little breeze riffling through the trees. It was growing late, and there was a magnificent sunset. And you know, the air didn't smell half bad.

When we got home, we didn't jump right into bed. We sat on the living room floor, rubbing each other's feet, listening to the Beatles' *Rubber Soul*, and talking about what a shame it was that Alan Freed had died penniless. Then Scott suggested I call my parents and invite them to dinner some night soon.

"Why, what's the matter," my mother demanded.

"Nothing's the matter," I said. "I just haven't seen you in a long time, and I miss you."

"She says she misses us," I heard my mother whisper, and immediately my father came on the phone and said, "Wendy? Wendy, what's wrong."

"What's wrong is that we don't get together more often," I said. "I'd like you and mother to come see me in my new place."

"She's got a new place," I heard my father tell my mother, and then my mother came back on and said, "We'd love to. When?"

So we made plans for an evening the following week. And I hung up feeling better than I had in a long time.

Then Scott took my hand and led me into the bedroom. But still we didn't get into bed. We looked at the picture of Dr. Holdsworth on the back cover of *Creating the Magic Within Yourself* and read the brief biography. Scott said he should have asked Dr. Holdsworth to autograph it before he went back in time. Then we started looking through some of Scott's books, talking about Vonnegut, Updike, and Twain, and trying to decide who our favorite American writer was. Scott said his was Steinbeck because his characters were so full of beauty, even when they were evil. I said I thought the final paragraph of *The Grapes of Wrath* was one of the most moving passages I'd ever read.

"I liked it, too," Scott said. And finally he took me into his arms and kissed me tenderly. I was glowing from head to toe. I felt like I'd been waiting my whole life to be kissed by him.

We made love, and it was fantastic. Afterwards, while we lay together loosely locked in a sweaty, exhausted embrace with our legs twisted together like roots of a tree, I said, "Just think - if those sorcerers hadn't gotten caught in a time warp, you and I would never have met."

"Oh, I think we would have, somehow," Scott said. We traded a few more tender kisses, and then we both drifted off to sleep.

CHAPTER FIVE

The next morning we woke up early, but got up late. Around noon Scott whipped up some pancakes, light and fluffy and covered with delicious syrup straight from Vermont. After that we went back to bed to work off some of the calories we'd just consumed. Scott had to be at the store late in the afternoon, and he just barely left in time.

As I watched him hurry down the street, I felt a fond little smile playing along my face. As soon as he disappeared, I cleaned up the apartment a little, then took a long, hot shower. I hated to wash Scott's kisses off my skin. But hey, I'd be getting more.

I got dressed, then headed for my place. On the way I passed a convenience store, and stopped in to get cigarettes; it seemed like I hadn't had one in ages. But instead of buying some, I decided it was time to give them up. It wouldn't be the first time, but I hoped it would be the last. And as I left the store, I felt incredibly healthy, the way you do when you've kicked a nasty habit. I concentrated on taking deep breaths. I recalled reading somewhere that we only use a fraction of our lung capacity, and that deep, full breaths are really good for you.

Before I knew it, I'd reached my apartment. I started to

let myself in, but then I remembered that Benjamin was staying there, and might not want to be disturbed. So I knocked timidly, hoping none of my friends would walk by and see me knocking on the door of my own apartment. There was no answer, so with my key I unlocked the door and let myself in. Taped to my refrigerator was a note that said, "Wendy - I've gone job hunting. Talk to you later. Benjamin."

Job hunting! I was proud of him. I took the note down and shoved it in my purse to show Scott later. Then I knelt down to study the spot on the kitchen floor that had been so ruthlessly torn apart not so long ago. It lay perfectly intact. A big bright square of sunlight poured in through the window, casting a cozy glow over everything.

"I'm going to miss this place, I can't believe I'm moving out, I can't believe I'm going to be living with Scott!" I murmured. My lease wasn't quite up yet, so I'd continue to pay rent for a few more months. But that was okay. Besides, if Benjamin got a job, he could take over the bills. And even if he couldn't, that was still okay. Scott and I would be together, and that was all that mattered to me.

I wandered into my bedroom and started going through all my stuff. I'm not a saver. I don't hang on to letters or even photographs. I threw out my college diploma two days after graduation, and all the pictures my classmates had given me, too. Nevertheless, there was a lot of junk to sift through. I came upon a box of religious pamphlets I'd collected when I was doing a piece on the evils of believing in God. Pretty juvenile stuff - He died for your sins and all that. I'd never believed in God, but at least now I believed in something. I guess I believed in myself, which to me was better than placing all your faith in some inaccessible Omniscient One.

But of course there was no point in putting down someone else's beliefs. I threw out all the pamphlets. Then I found a bunch of stories I'd written a couple of years ago. They were real cynical. I threw them out, too. I tore down the posters of my favorite Existentialists and crumpled them up. I even took down the painting Valentino had done for me, and set it out by the curb. Then I walked back to the convenience store and asked Mohammed if he had any boxes I could have, which he did, and which he generously gave me. When I returned to my apartment, I packed up all my books (no writer is emotionally capable of throwing out a book, no matter what the subject matter, for example, I still have my original copy of *Harriet The Spy*) and set them over near the door. Scott would help me move them later.

That was about it. I looked up and saw that the square of sunlight had moved across the floor into the living room. I rose stiffly, heaved a sigh, and helped myself to a beer - my last.

Just as I was cracking it open, Benjamin appeared at the door.

"Hey," I greeted him, "how did it go today?"

"Got a job," he said, grinning.

"Great! Doing what?"

"I'll be doing construction work on a new shelter for the homeless. Got a little experience with that."

"Congratulations," I said, handing him the beer. "Will you be staying here?"

"Unless you want to move back."

"No, I don't. I don't ever want to move back."

"Going to stay with Scott?"

"Yeah."

"That's great, I'm really happy for you, Wendy."

"Thanks." My face was pink with pleasure. I was so happy I was a little embarrassed. "Okay if I leave some stuff here for now? Scott and I will be by to pick it up some time later."

"Whatever you want."

"Good. Well, I'm on my way. I have a couple more errands to run."

We said goodbye and that we'd see each other later. Then I set off up the street. I knew that even though it was well after 7:00 the *Dirt* office would still be open. Blake could never seem to get to work before noon, and always wound up staying until late at night.

As I walked in, I looked with distaste at the Highway original hanging on the wall. I'd always taken a kind of perverse delight in its stark ugliness before, but suddenly all I was interested in now was beauty. I stopped and studied the painting, and I just didn't see the point of it anymore. Highway was certainly gifted at portraying the city at its most dismal, and this particular picture showed a drunken, grimy bum holding out his hand to a snotty, well dressed woman who breezes by him without even glancing his way. We're supposed to sympathize with the bum, Highway told Blake. He once claimed that the greatest minds in the country were living in the gutters of the city. I shook my head.

Then I heard Blake say, "Hey, Wendy! Got that Bedford piece done yet?"

"This painting is really terrible," I said. "It should be burned."

I turned to see Blake staring at me with a baffled expression on his face. I was secretly pleased. He's one of those guys who is really hard to surprise.

"What?"

"About the Bedford article. I read it about a zillion times. And you know something? He's right. Everything he says is right. It *is* time for us to take control and change things. And we're in a great position to do it, too. People read us. They pay attention to what we have to say. So from now on, we should start saying stuff that makes sense."

Blake was so completely dumbfounded that he dropped into a chair and stared at me.

"You serious?" he asked.

"You bet I am," I said. "We think we're being so sophisticated with our attitude, but we're really being childish. We're complaining about everything, like a kid who's unhappy at school but doesn't have the guts to confront his teacher. It's time we took charge of our lives and started enjoying ourselves."

"What the hell has gotten into you?" he demanded. I could feel his respect for me evaporate, but I didn't care. I no longer had the need to go around collecting respect. I was going to cultivate my own, and that was much more important.

"I've grown up," I said.

Blake didn't say anything for a couple of seconds.

"So unless you change the *Dirt* format, I won't be writing for you anymore," I added, and he looked so upset that I felt a little sorry for him. I used to be his best writer; my articles used to generate more hate mail than anyone else's on the whole staff. Of course I'd had a lot of admirers, too. But they were misguided admirers. I could see that now. "One more thing," I said. "I'm moving. I'd like you to come over and have dinner with us sometime."

"Us?"

"Me and Scott Bedford," I giggled. And before he could recover, I was out the door.

From there I went to South Station, and located the locker Dr. Holdsworth had rented. I used the key he'd given me to open it, and inside I found a thick stack of handwritten notes with the heading, "The more you believe, the more the forces of nature work with you and for you."

"Sounds like a good place to start," I said, hoisting out the transcripts and tucking them firmly under my arm. I was going to go back to our apartment, read through everything, and then call Elliot and tell him I had a much better idea for a novel.

ABOUT THE AUTHOR...

Although *Raising the Pentagon* is Robin L Stratton's first published novel, her professionally casual style suggests she's been at this for a long time. She credits her degree in psychology for her accuracy in describing characters in terms of action and motivation.

"When I sat down to write the book," she said, "I wanted it to be an indictment of people who point fingers at everyone but themselves. I also wanted to have magic as a theme. I wasn't sure how I'd combine the two ideas, but I think they blended together pretty well, and the result is a very upbeat, optimistic story."

If you enjoyed this book, watch for *The Dynamics of Flight*, the adventures of Lark DePaolo, a young ornithologist who goes on the road to confront life...but learns about death.

MOCKINGBIRD SQUARE